THE KILLING RAIN

JIM THOMSEN, EDITOR

THE KILLING RAIN
LEFT COAST CRIME
ANTHOLOGY 2024

DOWN & OUT
BOOKS

Down & Out Books
3959 Van Dyke Road, Suite 265
Lutz, FL 33558
DownAndOutBooks.com

Cover design by Bill Cameron

ISBN: 1-64396-362-7
ISBN-13: 978-1-64396-362-4

TABLE OF CONTENTS

To the late, great Seattle Mystery Bookshop,
just one more victim of serial economic murder.

FOREWORD
Megan Abbott

The 1974 conspiracy thriller classic *The Parallax View* begins with a surprisingly sunny, sweeping view from Seattle's Space Needle on Independence Day and culminates with the dramatic assassination of a U.S. Senator.

For the director, the great Alan J. Pakula, this setting was the ideal way to open a movie that speaks to the brooding disillusionment of the era—an America battered by Vietnam, social unrest and violence. The Space Needle, though built only a dozen years before for the World's Fair, represented a simpler, more hopeful time in the country. An "American totem," it suggested the Space Age, Camelot, a time that already seemed long-lost by the time of *The Parallax View*. "I wanted to start with Americana," Pakula said. "And I want to start with sunlit Americana, the America we've lost."

In many ways, Pakula's remarks speak to the contradictions of Seattle—contradictions that makes it the perfect setting for a crime novel. It's a city marked by remarkable natural beauty and yet also is a chilly monument to the promise of high-tech. It's a city known for both its liberal progressivism and—as Jim Thomsen notes in his introduction—its signature "Seattle Freeze" (not to mention more-than-its-fair-share of notorious serial killers).

Consider, too, its nickname—the Emerald City. What phrase

1

could conjure its contradiction more fully than the glorious place Dorothy seeks at the end of the Yellow Brick Road in *The Wizard of Oz*, only to find it's all a ruse, a concoction of a con artist and huckster?

With its heavy cloak of rain and mist, with its seaport history full of fortune-hunters, drifters, wanderers and anyone seeking to disappear, it's a city made for noir and Seattle's inherent contradictions (much like those of Los Angeles) only make it more so. As a little kid, I vividly remember watching a rerun of *The Night Strangler* (1973) on TV, starring one of my dad's favorite actors, Darren McGavin, as Kolchak, a reporter investigating a series of murders in Seattle. I still recall my gasps over the scenes set in the Seattle Underground, which, at the time, I believed was Hollywood fantasy.

Finally, about two years ago, I took a tour of the Seattle Underground, thrilling over its sunken wood gangplanks, its mysterious passageways, its distinctive, moldy smell, the strange feeling of seeing glimpses of the city moving above me, hearing the sounds of street traffic, life itself. *This*, I thought, *must be what it's like to be buried alive.*

It was in that moment that I remembered a line from *The Night Strangler*. "This isn't Fun Town, U.S.A.," Kolchak's editor tells him. "This is Seattle." The line made me laugh and it still does, but I won't soon forget the eerie feeling of being down there. A city buried under a city? It's a metaphor made literal, and a crime writer's dream.

MEGAN ABBOTT is a Left Coast Crime 2024 Guest of Honor and the author of several *New York Times* bestselling novels, most recently *Beware the Woman*. Originally from the Detroit area, she makes her home in New York City.

☂☂☂

INTRODUCTION
Jim Thomsen

W hen I was a boy, my parents often accused me of being "sneaky."

What could I say? I grew up in the perfect place for prime sneakitude: Bainbridge Island, a forty-minute ferry ride due west of downtown Seattle. Six miles away as the crow flies, but a million miles away as the crow breathes.

I spent long days in the deep, dark, heavily ravined woods behind our seemingly placid suburban neighborhood. Or skulking along the beach near the ferry terminal, creeping around creosote pilings, making notes like Harriet the Spy or Bob Andrews from *The Three Investigators*. I'd watch the boats come and go, their lighted windows making them seem like barges full of gold bullion gliding to and from the Emerald City, almost always half-shrouded by bridal trains of drifting mist. Often, I sneaked onto and around the ferries themselves. I kept countless caches of shoplifted candy bars, comic books and contraband reading (few things cheerfully warped my preteen brain more than *Helter Skelter*) the way, I suppose, serial killers kept favorite souvenirs.

At church, at school, at the places my parents worked, and seemingly everywhere in between, I left no doorknob unturned, no storage space unmined, no berry thickets or tree clusters left unexplored. Shadows were siren songs; locked doors were neon

Welcome signs; fences were calls to clamber over and explore. I was small for my age, a natural target for bullies, and this sneakiness was as much superpower survival skill as natural inclination.

Whenever I had ten bucks and a free weekend day, I'd hop the ferry to downtown Seattle, and walk portions of the city in a different four-square-block grid. This was the mid-1970s, and this was the Seattle of *McQ* and *The Parallax View* and *The Night Strangler* and *Cinderella Liberty*, not the Seattle of *Frasier* or *Grey's Anatomy*. Everything was pleasantly dirty. Porn shops and pawn shops and stanp-and-coin emporiums with sour-eyed old-men proprietors everywhere. Alleys full of still trash and moving shadows that rippled across puddles of rainwater. Every sidewalk seemed to inspire its own snaky Lalo Schifrin score, to pulse with overripe funkiness and the flat matte shine of implied menace.

I started doing this when I was ten years old, a shrimpy little blond boy alone in the big city, and it was only later that I realized that I probably could have and should have disappeared a dozen times over.

A few years later, I was a dormitory student at a Seventh-day Adventist boarding school, where seemingly every fun thing was against the rules. Rules, schmules: I faced that challenge with what felt a lifetime of training for it. I hid illicit radios and Walkmans and cassette tapes in light fixtures; I kept forbidden Stephen King paperbacks in a plastic sack I tied to a string of fishing line and slung up to the roof; I used a knotted rope, hidden in the hollow space of my dorm floor's dryer, for late-night shimmies out my third-floor window. Many was the night after lockup and lights-out that I sneaked out for two-mile strolls to the Piggly Wiggly—walking inside the edge of the woods alongside the road so that I wouldn't be spotted by any school faculty happening to drive past. I liked to pretend I was an escaped convict ducking from police dogs and helicopter searchlights, like David Janssen in *The Fugitive*, and the quote under my first yearbook picture was "A Quinn Martin Production. Act One."

Many, too, was the late night or early morning when, unable to sleep with my restless teenage demons, I sneaked out and stood under the dripping overhang of an outbuilding, staring off into the dismal dishrag of gray hanging over the Green River valley, sneaking puffs on an illicit cigarette. This was at a time when I later learned that serial killer Gary Ridgway, aka the Green River Killer, was just starting to prowl the nearby roads in his pickup truck in search of one of his many dozens of young victims. Good thing I wasn't a fit in his target demographic.

So, what could I say to my parents? My instinctive reply was also my truest:

"Sorry, but I was a product of my environment."

To live in the Puget Sound region is to live in a land of secret places: folds and draws and dense hollows and dark alleys and deep patches of woods between every housing development. And that's just close to the water. Go a few miles inland, and the houses get further apart; the fences get inviting gaps; the deserted barns and garages and buildings of businesses gone bust get more darkly enticing. There's always a tree or twenty to hide behind, a tall patch of weeds to flatten beneath, and a broken back window to crawl through and hide inside. And often, a layer of curdled marine-layer mist clinging to the ground for clever cover. And even more often, rain to wash away your tracks.

To live in this place is to live not just in fog but in shadow.

There's plenty of ancient two-tracks in the plentiful woods, smaller trails shooting off bigger ones; places were the trees grow so close together that you can stand beneath them in a biblical rainstorm and never get wet. Growth and gentrification has changed that to some extent—those woods behind my childhood home have been dozed and developed to one-percenty death—but the region is a place of people who are passionate about open space, particularly the kind devoted to

5

passive use. And that's all before you get to the mountains, to the tribal reservations, to the vast national parks, the long stretches of highways and secondary roads with suffocating woods ringed by snarls of ancient barbed wire stretching into seeming infinity. Places of beautiful scenery, pine-scented air, and seemingly malevolent rot stuffed into every square mile.

And even in the big cities—Seattle, Tacoma, Bellevue, Everett—you can find places to get happily lost before walking too many blocks. That urban grit of the 1970s I mentioned earlier? Really, the only change is above ground level; apart from the names on the shops and the sophisticated electronics that guard them, Seattle is still basically the same cheerfully crime-ridden craphole it ever was—in select sections at least, no matter how much sophistication has been slathered across its surfaces—and it scares the hell out of me after dark. And every time I'm in Seattle, on foot, after dark, I realize how much I love being scared. Even as my feet quicken their pace.

And I remember thinking, then almost as much as now, that these were all marvelous places for human dispatch and disposal.

They still are, and with that growth and gentrification has come a rise in reasons to create bodies in need of dumping: untenable economic disparities, battles over every undeveloped space, conflicts among litigation-happy neighbors over everything from fence lines to tree heights. The Seattle region is thought of as liberal, but that's true only until you get a few miles outside of the city. Then you're in red-state America—often the first sure sign is a sign urging the locals to vote NO on school bonds and levies—and it would be safe to assume the locals are as strapped as they are suspicious.

Unlike many other areas of the country, the non-Native American parts of the Puget Sound region are relatively unencumbered by white history, and therefore relatively unencumbered by suffocating notions of "legacy" or "heritage" or "tradition." We all came from somewhere else, whether it happened a hundred years ago or yesterday, and we rarely let our roots plant too deeply, or let them get tangled up with other root systems. For the most part, family names mean next to nothing here, and very few people are judged by them. Neighbors keep to themselves; on the residential street on which I've lived for five years, we greet each other with chin-nods instead of hand waves or spoken greetings, when we bother to acknowledge each other at all.

It's all in accordance with the social phenomenon known as the "Seattle Freeze," so named for the chilly reception we give to people who presume to breach our personal fences out of intrusive friendliness, and I'm here to tell you it is real (and that I practice it as an absolutely essential jungle-like form of protective camouflage).

Here, people are their own shadows.

Last summer, my next-door neighbor and I had a brief exchange about a wasp's nest on the divide between our properties. From eyes shrouded by the low pull of his ballcap, above a beard so full it seemed to have replaced his face, he told me that he had lived there for eight years, and that I was the first person on the street he'd spoken to in all that time. Nice guy, but until then I'd known him only as the guy who drove a black car with tinted windows and droned death metal of the sort associated with cinematic torture dungeons from behind the high-hedged walls late at night. For all I knew, he could have been keeping coeds chained in his basement and I wouldn't have had a clue; and, I admit, I could not have identified him in a police lineup.

The Puget Sound region, I realized, is the perfect place to disappear. In plain sight and otherwise.

Don't tell me that isn't fertile ground for murder. And fertile ground for *writing* about murder. And the fourteen stories you'll read after you turn this page are evidence of the fertile imaginations this place inspires.

T

OK, enough already with my blathering. Enjoy the stories that follow, and shake the hands of the many *The Killing Rain* authors in attendance at Left Coast Crime. And pray for rain (if it isn't already here). For none of us would be here if the killing I believe it inspires didn't dwell deep in our darkest hearts.

☂☂☂

THE LOVER OF EASTLAKE
Sam Wiebe

Saturday

Rachel Miles is in Seattle Children's Hospital tonight. The neonatal wing. She just had her baby. Not mine, of course — how could it be, she hasn't met me yet. But that's okay. A baby is acceptable to me. She and I have all the time in the world to start a family of our own.

What I'm prepared to do is not without risk. It's a crime, technically, stalking I guess you'd call it. My fate depends on Rachel and her reaction to me. I have faith in her, and faith in the grand romantic gesture.

According to the Rachel Miles fan site, she was born in Spokane (actually Ellensburg; the so-called fans always get it wrong). Youngest of three siblings and the family favorite. Her Wiki says her father was a commercial pilot and her mother a hairdresser.

It doesn't say that her father lost his job when she was twelve, and that by the time Rachel was seventeen and had her first modelling contract she was the family breadwinner.

It also doesn't say that Rachel's mother became a Christian fundamentalist. I learned that when I stopped by Mrs. Miles's home in Othello to deliver her lunch. Her parents are ordinary, but Rachel is special. I think a man who approaches her with love in his heart—laugh all you want—has more than a fighting chance.

Here goes.

☂

Monday. Crunches: 20, Situps: 20, Pushups: 10

I am not the most attractive or desirable man in the world. I'd estimate my looks as seven out of ten. Eight if I get myself in better shape. Cultural differences between us might raise or lower me in Rachel's estimation by a factor of one or two points. So, say six to nine, conservatively.

Rachel is a perfect ten, of course, even at the age of thirty-six. I believe my youth (twenty-seven) will be in my favor, since it indicates I have more sexual stamina to offer. That matters, even though I'm sure she'd never say so.

To improve my appearance, I've begun a low-impact, medium-intensity workout schedule. Crunches, sit-ups and push-ups every morning. Yoga or tai chi three times a week. I have subscribed to several YouTube channels with free beginner classes. Even with their commercial breaks, the workouts are a challenge.

I've also begun taking a supplement called Conqueror Root, a product derived from natural enzymes designed to increase virility. Once I am in the ideal shape, things will more readily fall into place. I would like to be in control. A shot caller.

Every day the gap shrinks between Rachel Miles and I. I'll soon be as appealing to her as she is to me, which is important. If we end up at her film premieres or fashion shows, I want to fit in with the other celebs. I want people to see me as deserving of Rachel. Or at least not seriously undeserving.

This is love, isn't it? Wanting to be the best version of oneself? I feel lighter than helium, yet solid as tempered steel. I'm in the process of becoming worthy.

☂

Wednesday. Crunches: 20, Situps: 20, Pushups: 12.5

One benefit of food delivery as a career is that I can go anywhere and fit in. Yesterday I popped into the neonatal wing at Seattle Children's with a curry in my warmer bag. I was questioned only when I reached the private area, and simply claimed confusion. It's a big building, after all, and it's easy to take a wrong turn.

It seems that Rachel had a complication with the birth of her son. Nothing life-threatening, both of them are fine, but I gather the baby has some sort of infection. He's being monitored for a few days, and she has remained with him.

This all seems to be an unnecessary precaution on her part. Her husband is older (forty-one) and maybe that accounts for the fragility of their offspring. Maybe it's because she doesn't love him, because he cheated on her, back when they were broken up for three months. I'm not an expert on reproduction or genetics, so I can't say for certain.

What I do know is that I got a glimpse of Rachel through the glass in the door of Private Room 16. She was in a simple blue gown, holding her son. My stepson, I should say, though maybe that's a little premature.

☂

Friday

Too preoccupied to work out today. Rachel went home Thursday night.

And I lost her.

I saw them go, that's the worst part. Rachel and the baby, her husband and her husband's assistant left in one car, with

11

Rachel's mother and older sister in the next. I followed at a respectful distance. Then I lost track of them around Montlake. I lost *her*.

One minute they were three car lengths ahead of me. Then there was a zipper merge, and they were six car lengths ahead, and then one lane over, and by the time I changed lanes they were turning down a side street. I doubled back, but there was no sign of either car.

Failure can't be excused. I must own this. That's why I went home and told my mother that I'd need privacy for the rest of the day. I have all sorts of old camping gear up in my room, including Dad's old Ka-Bar knife. When I was alone, I dragged the edge down the palm of my left hand and held out my arm with the fingers cupped so the blood pooled. I held it like that for five minutes. Good discipline, I think.

I don't know where Rachel is in this city. I know her husband is here directing some television show. Probably having another affair as well. While his wife sits at home with a possibly ill child, he goes on making his superhero junk, posing teenagers in costumes around Pike Place Market.

Last season I delivered to him on-set. They were filming in Elliott Bay. He and the others had worked through lunch, so I brought him poached salmon and fingerling potatoes, no butter, steamed broccoli with vegan cheese. His assistant ordered, technically, and I handed it to him, but I saw the young man pass his boss the biodegradable clamshell. Neither looked at me.

I ordered the same meal myself a few days later. Unfulfilling and wildly overpriced, but okay if you added hot sauce and a little margarine.

Today I brought Krispy Kremes to the set, paid for them myself, three dozen. I told the assistant I was allowed to say only that they were from "You-Know-Who." Movie people like little in-jokes. The assistant took the donuts and spread them on a collapsible table. I never saw Rachel's husband and I don't even know if he was on-set. They probably didn't save him a donut.

I know he will be here eventually, and maybe I could follow him back to her. But the set is heavily guarded. There are simply too many fans. How I hate them all. Loud, stupid, ugly, all crazy with emotion.

And I'm not feeling very charitable towards myself, either. I may have missed my chance at happiness. At true love. Worse, I may have ruined Rachel's chance at true love. I am a failure. Just worthless. I don't deserve her at all.

T

Monday

A big news day. This morning I read on *Collider* that Rachel Miles is set to star in a new spy thriller for Apple TV+, co-starring Chris Something from one of the Marvel things. "A feminist take on Bond" is how it's described. The director (not her husband, thankfully) is famous for making Hong Kong films with crazy stunts.

Filming will begin next fall, which means Rachel has eight months to regain her pre-pregnancy shape (34-24-34, 112 lbs.) and train. She will be extremely busy—I've read that after thirty, losing pregnancy weight is more challenging, and she's never done stunt work or fight choreography like this. Rachel and I are the same: we focus on something and go after it a million and ten percent. To win her heart I'll have to work fast before training becomes her sole focus.

The big news: I found my way in. Rachel's mother lives in Othello, and even though she'll probably be staying with Rachel to help with her new grandson, there might be a clue left in her house as to where Rachel is.

On TV, detectives break into houses all the time. I just need Rachel's address, nothing more. I'm not a thief and I don't want souvenirs. Information only.

I'll go early tomorrow, taking only my father's knife. This is a quest that the pure of heart alone can undertake. I will redeem us both.

☂

Tuesday

So, when I was in high school, I had this teacher who was really progressive. Her name was Mizz Reston. She once gave Ivan Danko and I detention for laughing during class. That was wrong, I think, since laughter is uncontrollable. Like punishing a sneeze. But Mizz Reston didn't hold that against me when I auditioned for our class play, *Macbeth* by William Shakespeare. She did change around the genders so the girls could do more parts, which I guess was fair since there were more girls in our class.

I got cast as Lady Macbeth. All I remember is holding my hands out and saying my big line, "Who knew the old woman had so much blood in her?" Mizz Reston didn't want us using paint or corn syrup and food coloring, and definitely not the real thing. So, I came onstage with clean hands and had to pretend.

Blood is way starchier than you'd think. It starts to dry almost instantly, like the skin on a pudding when it cools. It's gunky and hard to wash off, and it gets everywhere.

I broke into Mrs. Miles's house, no problem. The sliding door around the back was easy to shove until the little metal catch broke off. Then I was in the kitchen. When I delivered food to her that time, I'd seen the alarm panel on the wall. Opening the closet where the hot water heater was, I found the power source for the alarm, and was ready to rip it out. But a security company pamphlet had been tucked behind the cable, and the alarm code was penciled on the top. 05-04-88. Rachel's birthday.

Mrs. Miles is one of those old people who never got rid of her home phone or answering machine, but doesn't really use them, either. I checked her address book, and it had an address for Rachel from six years ago when she was still modeling in New York. No help at all. I couldn't figure out her computer password, and there was nothing written down in her desk.

Mrs. Miles will be my mother-in-law someday, so I don't think "Mom" would mind me snooping around. I found some naughty letters in her bedroom, but I'm not the judgy sort. Some gold and silver coins, too. Rachel's mother has some very nice dresses and shoes, probably presents from her daughter. There are a lot of framed pictures of Rachel on the wall, including one from her wedding. In the upstairs washroom there's even a photo of her with her old boyfriend, the drummer from that English band that keeps breaking up. The house is like a shrine to Rachel Miles. Ironic since Mrs. Miles is so religious, and "thou shalt have no other idols" and all that.

By the time I finished looking around the house, I was pretty despondent. And hungry, so I made some soup. My hope was that Mrs. Miles would come home, find me here, and listen to my case. A Christian would take pity on a truehearted lover and intervene. She'd been married before, and she'd raised Rachel, so some of that goodness must be in her as well. But Mrs. Miles never came home.

Instead, Rachel's husband's assistant came through the door while I was eating. I guess Mrs. Miles had given him the key. He saw me holding my spoon and he kind of bolted for the door, then stopped as if realizing he was the authority. He took out his phone and tapped it on his leg, asked what I was doing, said I needed to leave.

Understand, I never want to hurt anyone. I believe nonviolent solutions are most often the best. But my mission is sacred. It's holy—far holier than Mrs. Miles's pamphlets about how Jesus doesn't approve of certain marriages.

The assistant screamed before I even stabbed him and tried

to block me with his hands. Defensive wounds, they call them on *Forensic Files*. I gave him some more defensive wounds and he tried to run, but I held onto the collar of his jacket and get through the defense.

Poor guy. When I handed him the donuts the other day, he didn't look at me. I turned out to be the last thing he'd ever see. Poetic, I guess.

The assistant had two phones in his pocket. One of them was unlocked and had a chat going with Rachel's husband.

Sorry, I typed, what was the address again?

☂

Last Day

I took a shower before I left Mrs. Miles's home. That got most of the blood off. I had to borrow new clothes, a suit jacket I think was her husband's. Good sign that it fit me. I also took a Mariners hat, which squeezed my skull a little, but I got it on.

Rachel and the baby are staying on a houseboat in Eastlake, a rental. The street view shows a grid of floating homes, accessible by a series of gangplanks. The houseboats have big windows, and everyone can see everything. I've delivered around Lake Union many times. Parking will be the most difficult part.

The assistant had a fob for the gate leading down to the flotilla. I parked blocks away, walked over with the knife tucked in my windbreaker and the warmer bag slung over my arm. I wasn't nervous. Sure, I wished I'd had more time to work on my physique, and these were not ideal circumstances. But time was against me. This was the point where a leap of faith is required from the hero, even if he's unprepared. The leap *makes* him prepared. That's true in every culture's mythology and in every big-budget movie, according to a book I read. The end of the journey is always the same. Failure breeds success.

So it's time to leap.

I was a little disappointed when I saw Rachel's houseboat. They ranged from one to three stories, and hers was two, large but not the largest. The curtains were drawn. No one looked at me as I approached. Just another food courier. The front door was unlocked.

The ground floor of the houseboat had an open concept: living room and kitchen on the bottom, sweeping staircase, rooms up above. Mrs. Miles was the first person I saw. She smiled at me in confusion, holding a coffee filter and a plastic scoop.

"Are you supposed to be here, dear?" she asked.

I nodded and didn't stop to answer. Moving up the stairs, I came to an office with a view out over the water. The desk faced the window, and Rachel's husband was sitting there, on the phone, his back to me. He didn't look up.

I hesitated, thinking I should get rid of my rival now. Then I realized, no, Rachel must be allowed to choose. The director and I would fight after, for her honor, if it came to that. I moved on.

Running water from the end of the hall. A washroom with the door open, a shower stall inside. I saw her silhouette through the curtain and steam. A little pudgy from her pregnancy, but the back and profile could only be her. My Rachel.

I didn't leer or linger. That wouldn't be proper.

In the room next door, the bedroom, a cradle had been placed at the foot of the bed. The baby was sleeping there. Ugly little thing, red-faced and wearing a white cap. My stepson. A *Watchtower* lay on the nearby chair. I guess Mrs. Miles was watching the child while her daughter cleaned up but needed a cup of coffee.

I put down the warmer bag and lifted the little guy. Honestly, I don't know why I put him inside. You carry around this big red square with heat retaining lining, and everything you see you wonder how it would fit. One time I put a cat in there, but it made so much noise I let it out. My stepson would fit, with room to spare. He did fit. I began to zip him in.

Rachel. She was standing before me, in a towel, her hair a long slick trail down her neck. Staring at me and the bag and the crying child, astounded at the journey I'd made on her behalf.

I spoke from the heart. I said my name and that I'd come here on a mission of love, that she and I had been blessed with a chance at true companionship, a merging of spirits. I told her I was a good man, and would protect her, that I was virile, and every day getting better looking, and that *her* looks would fade one day but I wouldn't hold that against her, no, I would always be there for her, I was that kind of man.

Rachel looked at the bag, and at me, and ran into my arms.

Happily, Ever After

I'm a little confused as to what happened next. Rachel tripped, I think, and instead of embracing me she bent to pick up our boy. Who was fine but had started bawling. The noise made it hard to keep things straight.

She was comforting him, shutting him up so I could continue telling her about my mission. Her husband came in and shouted and hit me, and the knife fell out, and everyone gasped. I didn't pick it up because the only thing stronger than violence is love, and I'd armed myself with that. Her husband groped for the knife and picked it up and cut me. Pretty badly, it turned out.

I'm proud. No defensive wounds. If that doesn't prove my worthiness, nothing could. Passing out was regrettable, but not something I could control. Like the time I laughed in Mizz Reston's class, the body wants to do things whether the mind agrees or not.

I was in a hospital, then a cell, and then another hospital where I do nothing but answer questions all day. Interview after interview. I wonder if that's how Rachel feels when she's on a press tour. Something else we share.

The orderlies are nice and not too strict, and I have all the time I want to write to my love, and draw, and plan.

They tell me they mail my letters, but I doubt it. I think they're in some desk. No matter. A love letter is powerful. It's an entreaty from one heart to another. A love letter can't be deterred, only slowed down. Soon I'll leave this place to be with Rachel once again. Every moment is agony until that time, but it's a splendid agony because it's in service of something grand.

I pity people who don't have pure love to look forward to.

☂☂☂

CHASING DREAMS IN
THE EMERALD CITY
Cayce Osborne

April 26, 1962
9:35 a.m.

D etective Baxter Bell was in a foul mood for three reasons. The ongoing Century 21 Exposition—aka the World's Fair—was turning his beautiful city into a nightmare. Construction on the massive new Interstate 5 was cutting right through his neighborhood. And worst of all, his Girl Friday had quit two months ago, sauntering out the door in search of stardom. He was unable to find a replacement, and he hadn't solved a single case since.

The Bell Detective Agency—slogan: *Trouble? Give Bell a Ring!*—occupied a cramped two-room office in the heart of Seattle's Chinatown. Baxter was struggling with a new case, ready to bargain with the devil if it meant reversing his fortunes. Then Donna Davis hurried up the stairs and into the agency.

"Thought I told you never to show your face here again," Baxter growled, knowing it was Donna even before she spoke, because of her gardenia perfume and the click-clack of her high heels. He was seated behind his desk and refused to look up from his perusal of *The Seattle Times*, plastered with photos of the recently unveiled Space Needle.

Donna stood in his doorway, bouncy red curls a shiny halo around her face. She smoothed her emerald velvet dress over her curves, taking in the mess that had accumulated in her absence. The gray metal filing cabinet in the corner and the photographs of turn-of-the-century Puget Sound on the walls had acquired an impressive coating of dust. She could barely see Baxter through the towers of empty Chinese food cartons and boxes of DI•GEL antacid scattered across the desktop.

He wore his usual work uniform: white dress shirt with the sleeves rolled, skinny black tie loosely knotted, and gray wool slacks with a subtle houndstooth pattern. His salt-and-pepper hair had too much Brylcreem; the tracks the comb had traced that morning were still visible.

"Aw, you didn't really mean that, did you, hon? I've got such a nice face. Shame if you never got to see it again." Donna knew exactly how to charm her former boss. "I only quit because I was chasing my dream. Are you gonna hold that against me?" She pouted.

At hearing her voice Baxter felt a wave of profound relief, but he couldn't resist ribbing her a little. He searched the paper in front of him for the exact phrase he'd read earlier that morning. He found it under the headline: 'Girls of the Galaxy' showgirl revue shuttered after complaints.

"You mean to tell me your dream was to be, quote, a bare-breasted space girl cited for excessive shimmying and shaking?"

"Showbiz is the dream, Baxy. And the Expo is the biggest thing to hit Seattle since, well, the gold rush. I don't mind shaking my shimmy as long as I get to be up on stage."

"So, what, you chased your dream down to the Expo and it turned around and chased you right back?"

"They shut us down, just like the article said. What was I supposed to do?"

"Shake it somewhere else, I guess."

Donna summoned a single, glistening tear. She was a fantastic actress—a skill that had served the Bell Agency well over the years. "Golly. I don't have anywhere else to go, Baxy. Girls of the Galaxy was a once-in-a-lifetime opportunity. But since that's a bust, I thought maybe…You catch any good cases lately? Maybe something you could use me on?"

Baxter lit a cigarette and stared through the curling smoke at the woman he'd been half in love with for the last four years, and fully in love with for the last two. Realizing how damn good she was at her job was the clincher. Donna had him beat—and they both knew it.

And he did have a case, with zero idea how to crack it.

"You ain't getting your old job back," Baxter said, trying unsuccessfully to be the bad guy, leaning back in his chair and crossing his arms. "But I got a paying client. I'll give you twenty-five percent of the final fee, cash, if you'll help me solve it."

"Do tell." Donna cleared a corner of Baxter's desk and perched there, trying to avoid getting garlic sauce on her velvet dress—it was Baxter's favorite. She wore it whenever they needed to have a difficult conversation.

"Disappearance. Female. Friend reported her missing but the cops are so tied up with the damned Expo they ain't got the time to put in."

"A missing person," she said, bringing her hands together in two happy little claps. "Ooh, I'm good at those. I'll take your twenty-five percent and raise you. If we solve this thing, and you agree that I was indispensable to the investigation, you let me come back to work for a while."

Baxter stared up at the water-stained ceiling, not saying a word. That meant they had a deal.

Donna called down to Tai Tung's, the restaurant that occupied the ground floor of their building and ordered two chop sueys—one pork and tomato, one chicken and mushroom. While they waited for Quan to run their lunch upstairs, she straightened the office, listening as Baxter recited the basics of the case. Donna committed the following facts to memory, and she had an exceptionally good memory:

On the evening of April 23rd, two female friends attended The Amazing Dunninger's show at the Expo's Opera House. Isabel Smith, age thirty-four, sat in the audience and watched as her friend, Sariah McKell, age twenty-nine, was called up on stage to aid in a demonstration of mesmerism. After the show concluded, Isabel was told she could meet Sariah outside at the stage door. She waited there an hour before interrogating the unhelpful stage manager. Sariah never appeared. Security questioned those present but produced no results, and the police had no leads.

"I'd just as soon never set foot in that place," Baxter said, shaking his head in disgust. The Expo represented everything he despised: innovation, expansion, exploration, change. "But I'm sure you got contacts down there, yeah? We can get in and get out, quick-like?"

"Piece a cake, Baxy." Donna stood and rummaged in her crocodile shoulder bag, reapplying her lipstick: Guerlain's Rouge Diabolique, Marilyn Monroe's favorite. "We'll go down there and look around. Slip in the back door and be out in a jiffy, quick and painless."

"Good, good. Will you give the client a ring? Here's her number." Baxter shuffled papers around on his desk until he found a coffee-stained napkin with a scribbled phone number. Donna pinched it between two fingernails as if his mess might be contagious. "I want you to meet her. Have her come in as soon as she can get here. We'll head downtown after."

⟙

"Thank you for coming back in, Mrs. Smith."

Baxter took a large swallow from his steaming cup of coffee and leaned forward. Donna and the client sat opposite him, not touching their coffees, in a matching set of wooden lounge chairs that Donna had snapped up at a garage sale the previous summer.

"Miss, not Mrs." The woman pursed her lips as if the "Mrs." in her mouth had a sour taste.

"Come again?" Baxter had lost his train of thought.

Donna turned toward their client, wearing her most comforting smile—tucked chin, no teeth, eyes radiating calm. "Nice to meet you, Miss Smith. My name is Donna Davis and I'll be assisting Detective Bell in this matter."

The woman's lips trembled, her dam of propriety breaking. "Please!" Her voice was sharp with panic. "I need you to find Sariah. It's been days with no word."

"Detective Bell has given me the pertinent details, but can you think of any reason for your friend's disappearance, anything you haven't told us?"

"A reason?" The shine in her watery eyes turned desperate.

"Any enemies? A history of difficulties?" Baxter explained.

Miss Smith squirmed in her seat, crossing and uncrossing legs clad in a neat pair of burgundy dungarees. "No," she said eventually. "Nothing like that."

Donna switched tactics. "Why don't you tell us about her, then. Is your friend from Seattle? How did the two of you meet? What are her hobbies?"

"Well...we both moved to Seattle about ten years ago. Me, from San Bernardino and Sariah from Provo. Neither of us knew anyone here, and we became fast friends."

"Where did you meet?" Baxter asked.

"At the—at, um, a nightclub in Pioneer Square."

"A gal—like you—down there?" Baxter asked, his gaze jumping from her straight blond hair to her petal-pink lipstick to the lacy collar of her blouse.

Miss Smith half-rose from her chair in distress. When she realized she had no choice but to stay she sat down again, clutching a white cotton handkerchief in her lap.

"Mr. Bell is a good detective, but that does not prevent him from being an ignoramus from time to time," Donna said, patting Miss Smith's hand. "Please forgive him. Tell us more about how you met."

As soon as she'd composed herself, Miss Smith continued. "We both like to dance. She was an easy person to become friends with, at first because we had similar upbringings, but then because she's so outgoing. And brave. Two things I am not. I miss her so much." She brought the handkerchief to her face and dabbed at her tears. The monogram SMM was stitched in lavender thread in the corner of the cotton.

"Is your friend Sariah married?" Donna asked.

Miss Smith raised her eyes to Donna, and the two women exchanged a look. "No. We're both unmarried and intend to remain so." An understanding passed between them that Baxter was not privy to. Nor did he need to be. That's what Donna was for.

"Thank you for your time, Miss Smith," Donna said as she stood and moved to open the office door. "I think we have all we need. If you'll excuse me, I need to make a phone call. We'll be in touch."

When Miss Smith had left, Donna closed Baxter's office door, sat down at her own desk in the agency's waiting room, and picked up the telephone.

"Hello, Operator? I'd like to place an out-of-state call, please."

An hour later, Baxter parked his beat-up Chevy Bel Air in an alley off Fifth Avenue. He and Donna made their way on foot toward the Century 21 Exposition grounds. Show Street—the section of the Expo housing the now-dark theater where Donna had performed with the other Girls of the Galaxy—was two doors down from the Opera House where famous mentalist The Amazing Dunninger performed his act.

Donna weaved expertly through the crowds, dodging a fervent group of Mormons waving pamphlets, a sweaty man hand-selling cold bottles of Triple XXX Root Beer, and clots of gawking tourists. A bitter Baxter trudged along in her wake, pausing next to her as she knocked sharply at the back door of the Opera House. Donna stood aside. A huge bald man with a soggy cigar clamped between his teeth threw the door open, nearly knocking Baxter to the ground.

"Whaddaya want? I'm busy."

"I—we—um, we're here about the disappearance of, uh," Baxter paused to check his notes, "Sariah McKell, after the show on Monday night."

"Already told the police, I don't know nothin'." The stage manager was already closing the door when Donna stepped into view. A smile transformed his face from dour to delighted. "Ho-hey! Dazzlin' Donna! How ya been, kid? Sorry to hear about ya show gettin' canned."

"Aw, you know me. Like a kitty-cat, I always land on my feet." She swatted him playfully on the arm. "Say, Jocko, I've been helping my friend Baxter here look into that missing lady. Can you tell us what happened?"

Jocko gave her an anything-for-you smile. "Nothin' out of the ordinary on my end. She was invited up on stage by Dunninger, he did his hypnosis thing, snapped her out of it, and I helped her out this door. He don't like his volunteers to go sit back down in their seats after, on account of it distracting the rest of the audience. Very particular, this guy. I left her right here, safe n' sound, and got back to work."

"And the rest of the night was normal? You didn't see anything out of the ordinary?" Baxter asked.

"Nothin' is ordinary around here. A madhouse, I tell ya. But nah. Not like you mean."

"One last question," Baxter said, sensing Jocko was losing his patience. "What did you mean by Dunninger's *hypnosis thing*?"

"Every night, near the end of the show, he invites a volunteer up on stage and hypnotizes them into thinkin' they're somebody else."

"And who did Miss McKell think she was, Jocko?" Donna asked.

"The right honorable Mayor Gordon Clinton. See ya, kitty-cat."

The door shut in Baxter's face with a whump of musty air. He turned in a slow circle, eyes on the passersby, as if the teeming crowds held the answers he sought. Donna ignored him, her gaze focused on the ground.

"The way I figure," Baxter said in a listen-up-I'm-about-to-be-brilliant tone, "we have three possible scenarios. One, the hypnosis stuck and we'll find Miss McKell over at the mayor's house. Two, The Not-So-Amazing Dunninger cooked this whole thing up for publicity. Or three, Jocko has her tied up at his place—maybe a love-slave scenario."

Donna still had her eyes on the ground.

"Did you hear anything I just said?" Baxter asked.

"No."

"Okay, I'll take you through it again—"

She finally tore her gaze away from the pavement. "No! I meant *no*, as in, your theories are wrong. If she'd showed up at the mayor's house trying to get in, the police would've found her easy," Donna said.

There were raised voices in the crowd, where the Mormons and the soda pop man competed for customers, and Donna studied them, a smile blooming across her face. Baxter, despite being disgusted with his surroundings, thought she'd never looked more beautiful. "And I don't think Dunninger needs the publicity," she continued. "I've seen him on both Ed Sullivan and Jack Paar. It's a no for Jocko, too. He's a big ole grizzly but a softie when it comes to the ladies. Say—did Miss Smith give you a description of what her friend was wearing the night she disappeared?"

Baxter checked his notes. "A navy dress with gold buttons."

"And her shoes?"

"Um...saddle shoes."

"With tan soles or black soles?"

"Now why would a thing like that matter?" Baxter asked.

"Never you mind, Baxy." A light drizzle began to fall. "Say, why don't you go back to the office and relax. I'll finish up here. I have a few more people to talk to."

With a finger wave, Donna dissolved into the crowd. Baxter was left standing, hat in hand, wondering what in the world his assistant was up to. But he did as Donna asked, raising his trench coat collar against the rain and walking back to his car. Without noticing the twin black scuff marks on the pavement outside the stage door.

☂

As dusk fell, Donna returned to the office with celebratory burgers and shakes from Dick's Drive-In. She hung her vinyl raincoat and hat on the hook by the door, shaking a bit of moisture from her curls. She cleared Baxter's desk and set up their dinner. He was hunched over his food, devouring a Dick's Deluxe with extra relish, when he registered the mile-wide grin on her face.

"Whu?" he asked through a mouthful.

"Time to pay up, Baxy." Donna was seated opposite him, taking delicate bites of her dinner. In all their years of across-the-desk meals, rehashing an old case or debating a new one, he'd never once seen her spill or drop a bite. Donna Davis was on another level—out of his league, and he knew it.

He swallowed a half-chewed chunk of burger. "For the food? Just take it out of petty cash."

"Not for the food, silly, you owe me a cut of Miss Smith's fee, *and* I get to come back to work."

"When we've solved it—that was the deal."

"I did solve it."

"When? Where was I?" A glob of shredded lettuce, held together by melted cheese, plopped out of Baxter's sandwich and onto the desk in front of him. He didn't notice.

Donna had the grace to look sheepish. "I had most of it figured out while Miss Smith was here this morning. The handkerchief and Pioneer Square were what tipped me off. And their names, of course—a call to the temple in Provo sealed it. Then as soon as I saw the black marks and the pamphlet people, I figured out how it went down.

"While I was waiting for the burgers at Dick's I asked Peaches—he's the grill cook—if I could use the kitchen phone. I called and told Miss Smith everything. She said the soles were black, by the way. She'll drop off payment in full as soon as she gets back from her trip to rescue Miss McKell."

Baxter stared at her, mouth hanging open, his meal forgotten. "You better take me through it again. This time in English."

Donna took a long pull off her strawberry milkshake and stood, circling the small room as she talked.

"The first thing I noticed when you laid out the facts of the case were their names: Isabel and Sariah." Donna paused as if this should mean something to Baxter. It did not, and she continued. "Both names are out of the Book of Mormon—not many ladies are named in that book, so they stand out. Also, Miss Smith is from San Bernardino and Miss McKell is from Provo, two cities known for large Mormon populations.

"After Miss Smith left this morning I made a call to Provo and confirmed with the temple that there was a Sariah McKell, of the same age, run away and missing from Provo for some years. Her family has been very anxious to have her back."

"Family! So, she *is* married, and that's why Miss Smith went all zombie when you asked. She lied!"

Donna shook her head. "No, Miss McKell is not married. It's her father who wants her back so badly—a dreadful man, by the way. I asked her about marriage to give her an opportunity to indicate if, as I suspected, she and Miss Smith were a couple."

"What gave you that idea?" Baxter scoffed.

"Well, gee, lots of things." Donna ticked them off on her fingers. "The way Miss Smith was offended when you called her Mrs. The fact that they'd met in Pioneer Square—those nightclubs cater to the local homosexual populations. And the clincher: the handkerchief. It wasn't Miss Smith's—it belonged to her missing love. Didn't you notice the monogram? Giving someone your handkerchief is a romantic gesture, not a friendly one."

Baxter threw up his hands. "If you say so."

"Oh! And the marks outside the stage door. They were clearly made by someone dragged off against their will. Someone wearing black-soled saddle shoes, to be exact."

"So...what...her father found out where she'd run off to, came up here, and dragged her back home?"

Baxter's question wiped the triumphant smile off Donna's face.

"Something like that. I'm sure it wasn't easy for Miss McKell, growing up in a disapproving Mormon family as she discovered where her romantic tendencies were inclined. It makes sense that she'd want to run away and start a life somewhere more open-minded. Like Seattle. Her father finding her was all an unlucky coincidence.

"Mr. McKell, like thousands of other people, traveled here for the Expo. He and his church saw it as an opportunity to preach to the masses. You saw that group—the missionaries handing out pamphlets on Show Street? I talked to them, and they're from Provo too. Mr. McKell was here with them. He was at the Expo preaching to the unconverted and there she was, his wayward daughter, standing outside the stage door like the Lord himself had delivered her back to him. So, he took her. Because he thought it was his right." Donna's voice shook with anger.

"Huh" was all Baxter could say. He stayed silent for a good five minutes while Donna regained her composure. The milkshake helped. When she stopped pacing and sat back down in her chair, he knew it was safe to speak again.

"What do you think's gonna happen when Miss Smith goes down to Utah to find her...friend?" Baxter asked. "I doubt her family's just gonna let her walk away again."

"I was worried about that, too. Before I grabbed our dinner I stopped back by the Opera House and told Jocko all about it. He felt responsible—at least he did after I got him seeing things my way—and he volunteered to drive Miss Smith to Provo. He'll ensure Miss McKell will be able to return home safely. He used to be a bare-knuckle boxer and can handle any trouble they dish out. He was worried about losing his job, but I happened to know another stage manager who's currently out of work, due in part to my shimmy-shake, so he'll cover for Jocko at the Opera House for a few days. Easy peasy."

"Sure. Easy peasy." Baxter dropped his head into his hands. Donna walked over to pat him on the back.

"You woulda gotten there in another day or so, Baxy. I just hurried things along a little."

"But how..." Baxter began. He never understood how Donna connected the dots—except that she was always twelve dots ahead of everyone else.

"How'd I figure it out? I used to date a Mormon fella, back before I outgrew my gotta-get-married phase. So, I know a little about how they think." She slid a hand up Baxter's back to squeeze his shoulder, leaning down to whisper in his ear. "You wouldn't believe the things he wanted me to do."

"L-like what?" Baxter began to sweat, and hoped Donna wouldn't feel it through his cheap shirt.

Donna laughed, her breath a soft, strawberry-scented puff across his cheek. "His laundry, his dishes, and his vacuuming."

Baxter wanted to bang his head on the desk, but the remains of his dinner were in the way. He settled for a groan.

"You look like you could use some time alone, Baxy. And maybe a nap. I'll just go out front to my desk and find our next case. We'll need something to work on tomorrow—you know how I hate to sit around waiting. I heard a rumor at the Expo that the Paul Bunyan statue was stolen off the top of the world's largest birthday cake. Can you believe it? That just steams my buns!"

Donna would leave him again. This time, maybe, for good. But until that day, they'd take on as many cases as possible. The steady money would be nice, sure. But being by her side as she solved them would be sweeter than the chocolate milkshake currently melting all over his desk.

☂

Donna shut the office door behind her. Detective Baxter Bell reclined in his chair, sighed in contentment, and listened to the click of her heels and the drone of her faraway voice. Not even the I-5 construction noise could bother him anymore. He had his girl back—the most amazing, exhausting, brilliant person he'd ever known. He closed his eyes, imagining the delights those lucky audience members had experienced before Girls of the Galaxy was shuttered. Donna Davis shimmying and shaking? That was the stuff of Baxter's dreams.

☂ ☂ ☂

GUN IN HAND
Robby Henson

M axey Daltz drove east on Madison into a late October fog that had crept in off the Sound and reduced visibility to two car lengths in front of his Buick Riviera. His windshield was soon coated with drizzly wetness, and he needed his wipers and then even the palm of his hand to skim his side window, so as to safely make the sharp turn onto Pike. He'd had a client a few years back, a college professor, who told him that the ancient Greeks believed mist was created by some god (he forgot the name) to cloak the actions of mischievous spirits. Maxey had replied, "Must be why this city is so damn foggy."

Maxey slowed and flipped a turn signal as he reached 16th. Temple De Hirsch approached but only the ground level was visible, as the twin Mediterranean spires were obscured by mist. Maxey coughed a curse when he saw his usual Friday afternoon parking spot was taken by a station wagon with the back open. One of the reasons he timed his Friday visits with Rabbi Korn to a few minutes after five was that the loading zone directly in front of the Doric columns and twin temple stairs was legal for the taking and dependably empty. But not now. A couple of teenagers were unloading something out of a wood-paneled Rambler that most likely one had borrowed from a parent.

He parked halfway down the block and limped back, his hip and knees tightening from a combination of age, ample girth, and a fractured and repaired femur held together with screws from the shot that ended his career in law enforcement. It happened while he had been picking up side work as a bar bouncer on Aurora Street to help pay for his wife's surgeries. He had been three years shy of his pension when he shot the jaw off some drunken asshole who shot him first, but he had been let go with a severance and no pension or disability because of it. A lawyer he played cards with had said he could sue for more, and should, but he hadn't made up his mind on that, and seven years had come and gone, and he was still thinking about it.

But Maxey was doing all right, sort of, mostly.

He had sold his Mission-style bungalow in Whittier Heights after his wife passed. Most of what wasn't owed for her medical bills and funeral, he put into Boeing stock, and then had moved into two rooms in Phinney Ridge, bathroom down the hall, boozy landlady screaming for no reason and knocking on walls in the middle of the night. He worked a handful of jobs each month as a private detective and carried low overhead. The two hundred and fifty business cards he'd had printed six years ago hadn't all been handed out yet. Seven dollars a month for a listing in the Yellow Pages. He paid a service to take messages and he made his return calls from payphones. He would meet with prospective clients in diners and the closing line in his sales pitch was always the same: that he had worked fifteen years as a Seattle PD homicide detective, a fact that bolstered his otherwise unimpressive appearance but made him want to spit every time he mentioned it.

He limped back toward the temple, carrying a small brown sack spotted with condensation, and heard two seagulls squawking above him like they didn't get along. He looked up and saw nothing but swirling wet murk. Those unseen birds must be fighting and flying blind.

"Hey, mister, you got a light," said a kid leaning against the Rambler. Skinny as a rail and Maxey doubted if he had hit twenty. His slightly darker-than-coffee complexion and ample cheekbones said he had mixed race somewhere in his family tree. His pants were red velvet and pegged, and out of sorts with his dark suit top and thin tie. He held an open umbrella, but not above himself, over a guitar with a sculpted yellow body. His permed and wavy hair was getting the spritz and drizzle treatment. Three white kids in ties and jackets were struggling to lift a drum set and PA speakers up the marble stairs.

"Sorry, I don't smoke." Maxey did, but he didn't give out cigarettes.

"That's too bad. That your car, mister?" The kid nodded up the block at Maxey's two-toned Buick. Cream and tan. Barely visible in the fog. He must have noticed Maxey pass. "Nice ride, cost a lot?"

"Less than you think, Rivieras are the cheaper model, but it's just as flashy as the top of the line." Maxey didn't tend to chitchat with teenage strangers, but the kid's easy smile and youthful charm had coaxed it out of him.

"Sounds like my guitar." He nodded at what his umbrella protected. "It's flashy, but cheap. A Supro Ozark. "

"So you're a musician."

"I like to think so."

"Who do you listen to?"

"T-Bone Walker, Elvis. What's in the bag?"

Maxey held up his paper sack and was about to answer but one of the kids lugging gear told the skinny kid that he should talk less and help more.

Maxey found Rabbi Korn pushing a broom over the green tiles of the banquet hall in the basement. The double entrance door was propped open by two bricks so as to let the kids move equipment through and set up their amplifiers and drums on the small raised stage. The way they banged their stuff around and argued indicated to Maxey that they shouldn't count on careers in moving and delivery.

"We're having what the kids call a sock hop tonight. So I've only got five or ten minutes," said the rabbi. His kind eyes were deeply lined but always twinkled.

"Hey, do what you do, I'll circle back next week."

"What's in the bag?"

"Cinnamon rugelach."

"Not from that kosher place over in Seward Park?"

Maxey nodded and Rabbi Korn said maybe he needed a coffee break and left a pile of dust where it was on the floor and went to make a fresh pot in the kitchenette. Maxey followed. Rabbi Korn was reform, but he had married the daughter of a conservative rabbi and she had kept a kosher home and even pushed her husband into observing Shabbat. Since her passing he had backslid quite a bit. He still harbored a fondness for kosher rugelach, however.

"You're gonna need chaperones to guard the stairwells and punch bowl," Maxey said as the coffee percolated.

"Don't I know it. Esther's father had that part figured out. Strict separation by sex. He even had separate entrances."

"Where's the fun in that?" Maxey laid out the pastries on a paper napkin.

His end-of-the-week get-togethers with Rabbi Korn had become a ritual that Maxey looked forward to, as much as he looked forward to anything anymore. They had met by chance. Maxey had run out of gas during the grimmest part of his wife's illness, and he had walked twenty blocks to a Texaco and was pumping regular into a borrowed gas can when suddenly he was crying and moaning and Rabbi Korn had come up out of nowhere, seemingly, and put a hand on his shoulder when he needed one. Their conversation that started that early morning had led to more for more than half a dozen years. They talked about life, death, widowhood, sports, movies, and Maxey's profession. Rabbi Korn was an avid reader of pulp novels and a lover of Bogart movies and liked to pump Maxey for details of his job at hand.

"Nothing much to see, keep on walking," Maxey said when asked.

"Come on, give me something."

"A run-of-the-mill cheating wife stepping out on a brute of a husband. I snapped a few clandestine pics in the parking lot at the Leland Hotel, collected my pound of flesh, and went home."

"A yawner."

"Very much a yawner." That was the word Rabbi Korn had come up with to describe the private-eye jobs that lacked danger and excitement.

"The only thing outside the norm was the brute paid me in small bills and he snuck in some Mexican pesos in with the Uncle Sam greenbacks. I didn't notice until I was back in my car, so I had to climb out, and go back and knock to get paid in full."

"Did he confess to trying to cheat you?"

"Nope, he just looked kinda' punch drunk from what I had dropped on him, and all he said was he was sorry and had gotten his currencies confused. He did have a stack of Mex money on his counter."

"Was he Mexican?"

"Does Joesph Edelen sound Mexican?"

"Not much. But why all the pesos?"

Maxey shrugged. "He was a motorman on freighters, maybe his last port of call was Ensenada."

Suddenly the skinny kid started playing his guitar and went from dead stop to wailing crescendo in two seconds. His Supro Ozark was indeed flashy and so was the kid's playing, but the jangly notes icepicked Maxey's eardrums. Rabbi Korn clamped a hand over the side of his head and rose to yell at the kid to turn it down but one of his band mates had beaten the rabbi to the punch by yanking out the plug on the amplifier. That triggered a loud argument on the bandstand about how the guitarist always played too loud for the vocals.

The kids were still screaming at each other when two cops

walked in. One was uniformed. One was not. That shut the kids up.

The lead cop saw Rabbi Korn and Maxey in the opening to the kitchenette and came over that way. Maxey recognized him as Ju Ju Takera, almost forty, with Brylcreem-ed hair and a dark suit with subtle striping. He looked like a greeter at a funeral home. He had been handpicked by the captain of the West precinct in a push to make the Chinatown residents more comfortable with the face of the Seattle PD. Maxey had been in on his training. Then Takera had been partnered with a rival homicide detective who Maxey couldn't stand, and most of their conversations after that, and before Maxey had been let go, devolved into some kind of turf-pissing contest. Takera always tried to come across hard. Maxey figured he wore that to deflect digs at his ethnicity.

"Maxey Daltz, you down here repenting for your sins?" Takera said with an empty smile.

"No, I was waiting for your mother." Maxey could play his part too.

Takera turned to the beat cop, who was a thick side of red-faced beef and didn't seem like he would be handpicked by a captain for anything unless you needed somebody to curb-stomp another somebody.

"Daltz here thinks he's a funny guy. I can understand why he thinks that. The work he put in at the precinct was a joke."

Maxey burned eyeballs with the detective. Takera broke off the stare to look over the place.

"I knew you pinched pennies, but you never fessed up to being Jewish, what gives?"

"You wanna check if I'm cut?"

With a name like Maxey Daltz, he knew that many assumed he was a member of the tribe. He wasn't. His grandparents were Lutheran and Dutch and German. Rabbi Korn was of the belief that one of Maxey's ancestors, way back, had converted, as there was a lot of pressure to do that sort of thing back in the pogrom days.

"What can I help you with, officer?" Rabbi Korn interceded.

Takera ignored the rabbi and moved closer to Maxey. "Joe Edelen," he said, and reached down and picked up one of the flaky cinnamon rugelachs, leaving behind a grease spot on the napkin.

Maxey was hit with a bad feeling.

"Big burly seaman, lived in Everett with his cheating wife Mabel. He hire you?"

"I'm off the clock, I don't answer questions after five," Maxey said, but without any juice in it. He could smell where this was going. Takera, after all, was on the Homicide desk.

"Well, Joe killed her. Shot her dead." Takera paused to let that sink in and then unspooled the rest of the story to Rabbi Korn and ignored Maxey. "Mabel was stepping out, evidently. So Joe hired a keyhole-peeper to get the goods on her while he was out to sea. And the peeper came through in glossy, incriminating black-and-white. Boom. She got it this morning in her kitchen after she came home from the night shift at Boeing. Didn't even have a chance to change out of her coveralls."

Takera's story hit Maxey in the gut like a bucket of bricks. But he didn't flinch. He merely blinked and his head rolled back to last Saturday night: Mabel stepping out of some guy's Chrysler, she had bent down to touch up her red lips in the side mirror, smiling, giggling like a teenager, then she had sashayed in sky-blue high heels toward the hotel check-in.

Takera now took a bite of the kosher pastry, made a face like he didn't like it much, but swallowed anyway. He dropped what he hadn't eaten in a metal trash can and wiped his fingers on a Torah-scroll wall hanging.

"The sick bastard made her hold up your photo, the long lens one you took of her and her boyfriend at the Leland. He made her hold it up crying and moaning. She saw it coming. He put the full cylinder into her. The first two slugs pierced your photo and her chest, after that she must have dropped it, and the next four, she was on the floor. Side and back of the head. Your card was under a daisy magnet on the refrigerator."

"How did you track me here?"

"I'm off the clock, I don't answer questions after five."

"You get him?" Maxey asked. His voice was barely a whisper.

Takera let an uneasy silence grow after Maxey's feeble question until finally he said, "In the wind. He left his beater at the Vancouver ferry. Did he say anything to you about Canada? Any family or friends mentioned up there?"

Maxey shook his head.

"Did he say anything about anything that helps us find him? Mabel deserves justice, don't ya think?"

Mabel did but Maxey didn't answer. He looked at the wall at the other end of the banquet hall and the narrow window slits up near the ceiling and then his eyes dropped to the skinny guitar kid sitting cross-legged on the bandstand, listening to what the cop had said, his guitar not plugged in, but his fingers were chording patterns on the mostly silent fretboard.

Just then the drummer started banging out a few solo beats to tune his kit, and Takera told the red-faced cop to chase the band away. And he even had the moxie to tell Rabbi Korn to blow, in his own synagogue no less, so that he could come at Maxey with twenty or thirty more questions in private. And he did that. And when Takera was satisfied that Maxey was too thick and dumb to know anything that could help him, he made a few last-call degrading remarks about how private dicks were shit stains that did more harm than good and left.

Rabbi Korn came out of his office with sympathetic eyes. Maxey was slumped in a banquet chair and not moving.

"The man who pulled the trigger is to blame. No one else," Rabbi Korn said gently. He repeated what he said and tried to put his hand on Maxey's shoulder, but Maxey shook it off and stood and limped for the stairs, head bent, a sour taste in his mouth.

Turned out, this case was not a *yawner* after all.

Outside on the street, a boy and girl dressed up nice and looking about fourteen or fifteen, were getting dropped off by their parents for the sock hop. The girl had a pink carnation pinned to her lace-hemmed princess dress. The band was huddled inside the Rambler. That was all, except for the skinny guitar player who had found a cigarette from somebody and was leaning at the back end of the wagon where Maxey had first seen him. This time he had the umbrella over his head.

"What was that about?" the guitar kid asked. "With that cop?"

Maxey shrugged and the pins in his leg throbbed painfully. "Bad business."

"Sounded to me like some cat named Joe shot his wife and ran off to Canada."

Maxey shook his head slightly and reached into his pocket and pulled out a pack of Pall Malls. The pack was wrinkled and empty. "He didn't run off to Canada. That was just a feint."

"What do you mean?"

"He parked at the ferry to throw off the cops."

The kid nodded like he understood. "Where did he go?"

"Mexico."

Maxey could see that Ju Ju Takera had climbed into a black-and-white squad car with a bubble top that was backing out of a nearby driveway so he could turn around and head back past them.

Maxey was just about to step out into the street, flag down the red-faced driver, and spill it about the stack of pesos on Edelen's counter and his Ensenada theory. He should have given that in the basement. Mabel deserved justice. But the thing that stopped him in his tracks and kept him on the sidewalk was the raised middle finger pressed to the wet and drizzly window by an Asian-American homicide detective who Maxey had helped train and then come to despise.

The bubble top whooshed past.

"Good luck with your music, kid," Maxey said. He wadded

and crumpled his empty cigarette pack and tossed it at the squad car's receding taillights as it disappeared up Pike into the fog and swirling mist.

☂☂☂

PAYBACK
Bev Vincent

Ask anyone to describe a museum heist and they'll probably talk about a guy—always a guy—dressed in black rappelling from a compromised skylight, doing the limbo to avoid laser beams, dodging motion detectors, deploying drones or countermeasures to defeat security systems, which they've already hacked, replacing the live feed with something pre-recorded to fool the guy watching the monitors in a tiny, dark room in the museum's basement. *Mission Impossible* shit.

In reality, robbing a museum is much easier than that, especially if it's not the Tate or the Guggenheim.

My target was the Tacoma Art Museum, an unimaginative name dressed up by calling it the TAM, as if squeezing out seven syllables was too much to ask of anyone. Also, it helped that I wasn't after the Hope Diamond or a da Vinci, just a piece of cryptic art that was part of a collection touring the Pacific Northwest. I wasn't even after the centerpiece of the collection.

I usually worked with a partner, a guy named Bernie who'd recently spent several months in jail but was now back in circulation. When he didn't answer my texts, I decided to go ahead without him. A partner is good to have as a lookout or a getaway driver or someone who could take the fall if things went south, as they had during the incident that made Bernie a guest of the New Jail on Nollmeyer Lane, but I couldn't wait for him to respond. The exhibit opened on Sunday afternoon for a two-week run.

I decided to break in after closing on the first Friday. If they had hired special security for the collection—which I doubted—they would be more relaxed after several days without incident. That was the theory, anyway.

Cryptic art doesn't have the cachet of impressionism or realism or cubism or any other "ism." The idea is simple: there's something concealed in the work. Nothing so trivial as one of those 3D Magic Eye drawings that were all the rage for a while or a hidden-image puzzle where you have to find ten objects. The paintings and other works of art in the cryptic genre are crafty puzzles and there's often a reward for people who figure them out.

The centerpiece of this collection was by an artist named Luke Kelling. By combining clues from "Fools Gold" and eight other paintings, people were supposed to figure out the location of a treasure reportedly worth half a million dollars. I suspected—given that Kelling's net worth was more in the five-figure neighborhood than six or seven—that the treasure hunt was a hoax. I also suspected that the title of this piece was a clue to that fact. However, given that the treasure hunters were scouring three states to find it, often trespassing or otherwise disturbing residents and wildlife, mine was clearly a minority opinion.

Maybe...maybe not. I cared nothing about Kelling's entry in the exhibition. I was only interested in Hugo Ellison's untitled painting. It contained a puzzle that had defied experts and amateurs alike for three decades, but I had turned up the key. The painting itself was only part of the equation. A couple of years ago, I had stumbled upon Ellison's handwritten journal while I was...well, let's just say "otherwise engaged." From it I learned there were clues in parts of the work not generally reproduced in catalogs or web pages, including the frame and the back of the painting. After reading and rereading the journal, I was ready to test my theories on the artwork itself—but I needed to have it in my possession. Staring at the painting on a museum wall wasn't enough.

The reward? I had no idea. Supposedly valuable and certain to have appreciated in the thirty-three years since the painting first went on display.

As I said, breaking into a museum isn't usually all that hard. All I had to do was get my hands on a key card that also disabled the alarms. That required social engineering, which is something I'm pretty good at.

The crowd at the exhibit opening that Sunday afternoon was larger than I expected for such an esoteric collection. The TAM must have done a good job promoting it. I wouldn't know—I'm not on their mailing list. I joined the gawkers clustered around the Kelling, then stepped away to take in the other paintings and *objets d'art*. Trying not to appear conspicuous, I gradually made my way to the corner where the Ellison painting was on display.

While I studied it, I casually surveyed the room, making note of the staff working the exhibit. I know men find me attractive, a fact I've often used to my advantage. Shamelessly. They used to call us the weaker sex, but it's so easy to wrap a man around my finger I question that conventional wisdom.

This time, I didn't even have to make the first move. A man in a dark blue blazer and powder-blue polka dot tie was sizing me up. Our eyes met and I held the gaze a little longer than necessary before turning away. He was older than me, maybe forty, and didn't sport a wedding ring. That was good. Married men pose more of a challenge sometimes.

I lingered in front of the work adjacent to the Ellison, well away from the crowd at the Kelling. I didn't have to pretend to be puzzled. I couldn't make hide nor hair of the painting, which looked like a collision of styles between Picasso, Pollock, and my sister's four-year-old daughter. I stood there long enough for Mr. Blue Blazer—his nametag identified him as Timothy—to come over and attempt to explain the inexplicable hanging on the wall before us.

I pretended to see what he was getting at, but with each passing moment I grew more convinced that he had no more idea what the loops and swirls on the canvas meant than I did. Still, I gave him my full attention, turned on my charm, and made myself as memorable as possible. I thanked him profusely for his insights, resting a hand on the sleeve of his blazer as I did so. Then I released him to attend to the other patrons, but I made sure he saw me looking at him a few more times before I left.

The TAM was closed on Mondays and Tuesdays. The crowd was smaller on Wednesday afternoon than it had been on Sunday, but still large enough to tell me they weren't wasting their time hosting such an odd exhibit. Timothy saw me inspecting a painting that the guidebook claimed concealed the identity of an unknown heir to the British monarchy. He wandered over nonchalantly and struck up a conversation.

When the museum closed at five, we had drinks at Bar960 in the lobby of Hotel Murano, not far from the TAM. Over glasses of chardonnay, Timothy regaled me with trivia, including the fact that the bar's name referred to the temperature of glass-cooling ovens. The walls and ceiling of the hotel lobby were festooned with works of art, but I got the idea Timothy was more interested in the hotel's guest rooms and the beds they contained. I was confident I had him on the hook. When I asked if he'd be at the TAM on Friday, he nodded quickly. If he wasn't on the schedule already, I was certain he would trade with someone else to work that shift.

That Friday, I wore one of my favorite little back dresses, accompanied by a rhinestone tassel necklace with matching bracelet and earrings. Timothy met me at the gallery door and followed me around like a puppy dog until he realized he was ignoring some of the distinguished patrons in attendance. He excused himself, explaining he had to make sure the moneybags were satisfied, his exit line accompanied by an awkward wink he probably intended to be salacious.

He didn't realize I'd relieved him of the keycard he kept in his blazer pocket. I'd observed him putting it there when we left the museum on Wednesday afternoon. I replaced it with a replica to keep him from noticing its absence.

A while later, I pulled him aside and asked if he could get away early. This was crucial. If he had to lock up, he would notice the missing keycard. I pressed myself against him and whispered in his ear. He agreed without hesitation, saying he'd get Marlene to close.

I left at four thirty, half an hour before the gallery closed, telling Timothy I wanted to freshen up before meeting him at the bar. He tried to act cool, but he seemed excited by the prospect. I suggested he get to the bar as soon as possible to save us a place because it was bound to be busy on a Friday. He nodded. Did I feel a twinge of guilt knowing he'd wait for me for quite a while before he realized I wasn't coming? Maybe a little. He was a nice enough fellow. Maybe he'd meet someone else at the bar.

I changed out of my LBD and into my prowling uniform. Yes, it was all black: jeans, sweater, sneakers and watch cap. I parked in front of Zeeks Pizza and waited until I was sure the cleaning crew were done for the evening, then headed up the street, sticking to the shadows, and approached a side door. The key worked on the lock, and a second swipe in front of the alarm console deactivated the security system. I marched into the main gallery and headed straight to the far corner, then stopped.

The Ellison was gone.

All the other paintings hung in their appointed positions, but there was a gap on the wall beside the title card that described the painting I coveted—the painting I was there to steal. I was stunned. Could they have taken it somewhere to be cleaned or repaired? It had been there only a couple of hours earlier.

I was stunned. I didn't understand.

I was still standing there, jaw slack, when I heard a sound at the front door. I stepped into a shadow and saw that it was Timothy, accompanied by several police officers. He didn't bother trying his replica keycard. Instead, he punched a code into the console beside the door. I looked around, hoping to find a way out. That was when I noticed the rope dangling from the skylight. For a second, I considered climbing it, but it was too late. The police were inside, and I had no choice but to surrender.

The district attorney threatened to charge me with stealing the Ellison, which the gallery had insured for half a million dollars, but I have a good lawyer on retainer. It was clear I hadn't stolen the painting because I was still in the TAM when the cops arrived, and the painting wasn't. I had purloined the keycard, so why would I need to force open the skylight to gain access to the museum? The D.A. suggested I'd been working with an accessory. After all, what were the odds of two people breaking into a place at the same time, he asked with a smirk.

"One hundred percent, apparently," my clever and well-remunerated lawyer responded.

Finally, they hammered out a plea deal. I admitted to criminal trespass, for which I received a six-month sentence at the Pierce County jail, three months of which were suspended, and a $1,000 fine.

While in lockup, I had time to reflect on what had happened that Friday evening. Who could have known I'd be breaking into the TAM and what I was after? I couldn't remember mentioning Ellison to Bernie, but I might have. It seemed suspicious that I hadn't been able to get in touch with him and that he'd made no effort to contact me after my arrest. I'd visited *him* in jail.

After I was released, I discovered my apartment in Fern Hill had been ransacked. The only thing missing was the journal needed to decode the painting.

A friend of a friend who owed me a favor reported seeing Bernie a few times at a nightclub in McKinley Hill. I staked the place out for three nights in a row until I saw him heading toward the building with another man. A familiar man, even though he wasn't wearing a blue blazer.

Timothy from the TAM!

From the way they were interacting, they seemed like more than casual acquaintances. My internet search for the nightclub confirmed my suspicions. My feminine wiles had been wasted on Timothy. He'd been in cahoots with my old partner so I'd take the fall for the robbery. I guess Bernie hadn't gotten over the fact that he'd gone to jail after one of our operations didn't work out the way we'd hoped.

For a moment, I thought—okay, that was payback. I had accidentally tripped a silent alarm but only he had been scooped up by the cops. Turnabout is fair play, after all. However, I hadn't then looted Bernie's place while he was behind bars.

I didn't know where he was living these days, so I followed him home after he staggered out of the club shortly after midnight. After he entered an apartment building ten blocks away, I found one of his aliases on the list of residents next to the buzzers.

The next evening, Bernie and Timothy were back at the bar. When they went inside, I returned to his building. The outer door wasn't firmly closed, and I made short work of the lock on his apartment. It wasn't a big place—one bedroom, one bathroom and a living room-kitchen-dining room defined by the way the furniture was positioned. The Ellison wasn't hanging on any of the walls, nor was the artist's journal on a bookshelf, but I hadn't expected they would be. It didn't take long to confirm they weren't anywhere else in the apartment, either. I left as quietly as I'd come, making sure there was no sign of my presence to tip off my now-former partner.

That left Timothy, the clever curator from the TAM. It made sense for him to have the stolen items. He would have better connections to sell them on the black market, if that was the plan. I couldn't see Bernie trying to solve the puzzle, either. He was more interested in making a quick buck. But Timothy? He'd already demonstrated that he knew a lot about the cryptic artwork on display at the gallery. I hoped he hadn't already sold the painting.

I got back to the bar in McKinley Hill in time to see Timothy offer Bernie a warm embrace before getting into an Audi Quattro delivered to the entrance by a valet. It wasn't obvious who was social engineering whom.

I followed him to an upscale neighborhood in the North End. He parked the car in a garage attached to a Craftsman-style house, then went inside. I watched from across the street until the lights went off. I made a quick circuit of the house to check it out, then jimmied open a window at the back. No alarms blared, although I knew all too well the risks of silent alarms, so I went straight to the front door to check the console. The display said DISARMED.

My night vision has always been an asset in my chosen profession, and it served me well as I made my way through the dark, one-story house. I figured the master bedroom would be at the far end from the garage, and my instincts proved correct. I could hear gentle snoring as I approached the open bedroom door.

Timothy was considerably bigger than me, but I had an equalizer—my trusty stun gun, the only weapon I ever carried. Fortunately, I hadn't had it with me the night I was arrested at the TAM, or I would likely still be sitting in jail.

I'd never used it on someone who was asleep before, but I needed to maintain the upper hand. I threw back the bedcovers and gave him a jolt that zapped him awake but left him dazed, disoriented and in significant discomfort. I used this brief advantage to zip-tie his wrists, then his ankles. I also put a strip of Gorilla Tape across his mouth in case he decided to start screaming.

While he recovered, I made a quick survey of the house. I found what I was looking for in a small room Timothy had converted into a home office. The Ellison painting was leaning against the wall and the artist's journal was open on his desk next to a pad on which Timothy had written pages of notes. He'd had a few months to work on the puzzle but, from a perusal of the notepad, it didn't look like he'd gotten very far.

I put the journal and the notepad in my backpack and carried the painting with me when I returned to the bedroom. Timothy glared at me. I was wearing a ski mask, but I was sure he recognized me.

"Timothy, Timothy," I said. "You've been a bad man."

He struggled for a few seconds before realizing he wasn't going to be able to break the zip ties. I indicated the painting. "Wouldn't your boss at the TAM be interested to know where this went? Or the police. The insurers and the owner, too, come to think of it."

Timothy kept glaring at me.

"Once I figure out the puzzle, I plan to give it back. I didn't intend to steal it—only borrow it, really." I paused. "Your fingerprints are all over it, I assume."

He frowned.

"Maybe Bernie's too?"

Realization dawned.

"Don't worry. I'll preserve the evidence. Ta ta!"

I left the way I'd come in. Once I was in my car, I left a message on Bernie's phone, saying he should check on his boyfriend. I didn't want Timothy to starve.

If I went back to my apartment, it wouldn't be long before someone came looking for me. Time to get out of town for a while. Everything of value I owned was in my car's trunk, and the Ellison painting was nestled in a blanket behind the passenger seat. I jumped on I-5 and headed north toward Sea-Tac. I had a one-bedroom apartment in Yarrow Point no one knew about where I sometimes laid low after a big score. A nice, quiet place to work on the Ellison puzzle.

And, yes, I did plan to give the painting back when I was done with it, fingerprints and all. You know what they say about paybacks.

�ూ☂☂

THE BARNUM DOCTRINE
dbschlosser

I always count on lousy weather during my annual beach
retreat with my wife, so our trips are never ruined.

I never count on a corpse.

I watched as several weatherproofed teens half-circled it. I
listened to their sobs and electronic shutter clicks as they cycled
to and from the body, denying and confirming.

Their adult slumped twenty yards distant, head hanging. He
shouted a hoarse admonition to his group to stay away, to wait
for the police.

They did what my limited exposure to teens suggested they
would do, which was to ignore him.

Brigid stroked her long red curls into her I-mean-it ponytail.
She nudged me toward the minder and veered to the body.

"Can we help?" I said to him. "My wife's a doctor." I chose
not to complicate the conversation by qualifying that she's a
veterinary doctor.

"What?" The man's face draped off his skull as if he were
decades older than what I guessed was mid-thirties, a few years
younger than we were. "Who?"

"My name's Parker Glynn."

"I—my class. Like that. We found her."

Brigid crouched over the body. Touched the wrist, the
throat.

"We're staying at the lodge." I pointed to our cabin. "What can I do for you?"

"Already." He showed his phone. "I called."

I left him mumbling and crossed to his students. Brigid had moved them back a few paces. The girls whispered and pointed, sniffled and comforted. The boys puffed and gawked, prodded and dared.

"Before the police get here," I told them, "you need to move over there."

They gaped.

"By your teacher."

Glad our pistols are under our coats instead of freaking them out even more. I looked to Brigid, who gave a quick shake of her head.

I took a step toward their teacher. "Over there."

I herded them. They shuffled. Some leaned over and touched their teacher.

I returned to Brigid. "You okay?"

She wouldn't look up. "We passed her."

"It was dark."

Our vacation ritual was a daily pre-dawn walk to watch the sunrise as it revealed La Push's ethereal sea stacks, tiny tree-topped islands hovering among twisting fog and churning surf. I surveyed our earlier footprints, closer to the ocean for firmer sand. They stood out under the watery light peculiar to the Pacific Northwest, a cloudy daylight diffusion that's not gloomy, but not exactly sunny, either.

"When we went by," I continued. "Could have done something?"

"Just kept them—" Brigid watched the students. "Those kids know her. From school." She motioned at the wood and weed tracing high tide above the body. "They came for biology class, low tide at seven thirty or eight."

"Can you tell what happened?"

"Not my practice area." She pointed at the dead girl's neck.

"But I see that."

The diameter of a pencil and black against the blanched skin, twin punctures over her jugular.

☂

Until stumbling on a vampirically wounded corpse, we had not appreciated our lodge's proximity to Forks. My wife loved our November week away from our home in the northern Rockies on the northern coast of Washington for its solitude.

Which evaporated after a dozen teens posted to TikTok and Instagram images of a dead girl.

A dead girl with what appeared to be bite marks on her neck from the real-life setting of the *Twilight* novels and films.

The Quileute tribal emergency management car arrived seconds before a Clallam County Sheriff's deputy, who staked out a square around the body using yellow tape and driftwood that I pounded into the sand for him .

"Thanks for moving the kids away from the body," he'd said.

"I've got some crime scene experience," I'd said.

The deputy announced that I was his new deputy.

"How'd you learn crime scenes?" He wrapped tape around a thick branch I steadied for him.

"I'm the city and county manager back home." I packed rocks around the base of the branch. "Small place. My wife and I end up helping out sometimes."

"She's a doc?" He glanced at his car, where Brigid sat writing her statement.

"Veterinarian. But she takes care of me if I need anything short of the ER."

The deputy grunted as he tied off another corner. "You can take care of me until the other deputy on this side of the peninsula shows up. And it'll be a couple of hours before the detective gets here from Port Angeles."

Parents began arriving for their children. The deputy said, "If you've got enough command presence to keep those kids from leaving, I could take pictures before I get their statements."

"Command presence is my middle name," I said.

I told parents to wait with their children in individual cars to keep the students from confusing each other's memories. I settled the two kids whose parents had not yet arrived in the first-responder cars.

The second deputy rolled up in time to restrain a shrieking, flailing woman I assumed was the dead girl's mother. Other parents embraced her, took her out of sight.

I applied my lawyerly eye to Brigid's statement, holding her hand inside my coat pocket for contact and comfort. Then we crossed to where the teacher sat, unmoved since we'd arrived.

"Parker Glynn," I reminded him.

When he nodded, his jaw drooped even lower against his chest. "This is Brigid."

He raised his head, then twisted to watch the arriving ambulance. "Did—" He looked back to Brigid. "You checked?"

"You knew her?" Brigid's clinical voice.

The teacher's eyes bugged. "Knew? Ashley—no, I didn't."

He scrambled to his feet. "I mean, she's a student."

He spun, stopping when he faced the body. "At Forks—was."

He made a half circle so he faced away. "Not my student. I mean, she used to be. Ashley Hagen. Last year."

He clutched my hand. "Glenn, you said?" Shook it with vigor I found surprising, considering he'd been catatonic for the past half hour.

"Parker Glynn." I tried to extricate my hand. "And Brigid."

"I'm Mr. Bingley." He started for Brigid's hand. "Charles Bingley."

Brigid inserted her hands in her coat. "You knew Ashley."

"Could you—you know—tell?"

Brigid cocked her head. "What."

Bingley watched EMTs slide a gurney from the ambulance. "What happened?"

"I only checked for a pulse."

"So you couldn't—oh, God."

I followed his eyes to a big SUV wrapped in Discover Forks signage. A woman drove. She parked next to the sheriff's cars.

When I looked back, Bingley was trudging toward the SUV.

I took Brigid's hand from her pocket. "Well."

"Yeah," she said. "Totally."

꙳

The detective found us in our cabin, where we'd returned after the deputy explained that the woman in the SUV was the tourism director at Forks Chamber of Commerce. "The crazy chick behind all this vampire and werewolf bullshit," he'd called her. We'd watched Bingley exchange tense gestures and indistinct strident words with her.

Detective Prager was a sturdy mid-fifties woman with efficient hair and outdoor clothes sporting a profusion of pockets. She handed over business cards when she shook our hands, then sat in the chair beside the whispering gas fire.

"Deputies said you were helpful."

Her tone did not indicate gratitude.

"They had their hands full," I said as we took the couch. "And we recently had some experience back—"

"Heard all about it. My sheriff talked to your sheriff. Your sheriff told mine you're not likely to fuck anything up too bad."

"Your sheriff's words, I'm sure."

Prager checked her notebook. "Hard to say." Clicked her pen, looked at Brigid. "You messed with my body."

Brigid surprised me by remaining studiously neutral. "I checked for a pulse. First on the wrist, then on the neck."

"That's it?"

"That's it."

"Where else?"

"That's. It."

Prager looked at me. "She's a doctor?"

Brigid started to reply. I stopped her with a touch on her knee. "My wife is a veterinarian."

"So, not a real doctor."

Rookie mistake.

"I studied medicine longer than your physician." Brigid glared at the detective. "I could recommend a prescription to clear up that skin condition."

Prager's hand dashed to a scaly red patch near her left ear.

"Assuming your GP hasn't already biopsied it to make sure it's not pre-cancerous."

"You've made your point, Doctor Glynn." Prager used the hand that had betrayed her to point at me. "And how did you contaminate my crime scene?"

"I moved a dozen teenagers, who'd been standing around the body taking pictures for fifteen or twenty minutes, outside the perimeter I helped the deputy secure."

"Pictures." Prager made a note, shook her head. "Mother of God."

When Brigid had gone to the bathroom an hour earlier, I'd sneaked a look at headlines on my phone. The top-center story linked to a *Seattle Times* article about a "rumors of *Twilight*'s vampire killer going viral."

Prager looked from me to Brigid, then fixed on me. "You gonna quit with the lawyer act?"

"You gonna quit with the bad-cop act?"

Prager studied her notebook for several seconds, then looked through the window toward the ocean. "We don't get many of these." She blinked repeatedly. "My daughter's the same age as Ash—as, uh, the victim. High school senior."

We considered the pre-teen daughter of Brigid's best friend as our own. All of us had read *Twilight* during her mercifully brief vampire-love phase. Brigid hooked a finger through one of my belt loops and tugged.

"We've got one, too," I said.

Prager looked at Brigid. "Can you make any guesses?"

"I shouldn't."

"It's two hours back to the coroner's office. Another day for the autopsy, if I'm lucky. Ashley can't wait that long."

Brigid took two deep breaths. I smelled her cinnamon toothpaste. She unhooked her finger.

"The neck wounds didn't have anything to do with her death," she said. "Shallow, and not much blood. Probably postmortem."

"What about the"—Prager flipped a page in her notebook—"bruises on her wrist you put in your statement?"

"Pre-mortem. That's all I could say. I only saw one wrist."

Prager scribbled. "What else?"

"I'd be guessing."

"Your guesses are better than anything else I've got right now."

Brigid set her jaw, then shook her head. "Her skin was the same temperature as the sand, so she'd been there at least a few hours. She wasn't soaked—just splashed, like from a wave—so she was left there after high tide. Maybe one or two this morning."

"Any sign of what killed her?"

Brigid put her palms inside her knees, rocked a little. "I don't—"

"Anything," Prager urged. "Please."

"Her lips were blue. Cyanotic. Not from the cold."

Scribbling.

"But there weren't any bruises around her throat, so she might—" Brigid scooted away from me. "This sort of guesswork is wrong."

"Please." A whisper.

Brigid looked away from Prager, from me. "She might have

choked. Sat in the garage with the car running. Somebody might have just dumped her body there. Not killed."

Prager looked up from her notebook.

"What makes you say that?"

Brigid twisted her fingers in knots and plucked them apart.

I reached across the couch to take one of her clenched hands.

"I think she was pregnant."

☂

I steeped tea while Brigid repeatedly and hotly told Prager that she had not compromised the crime scene by physically examining Ashley's body. She based her pregnancy guess on the behavior of Ashley's teacher, Bingley.

When Brigid excused herself for the time-out that I knew she needed, Prager and I took our drinks to the patio. I savored the monotonous rumble of the ocean, the earthy scent of my tea, as Prager reviewed her notes.

"I don't know if any of her guesses are right," she said, "but you two gave me more information than both deputies."

"Guesses aren't information." I sipped from a Team Jacob mug and looked west.

"Is she right?"

"I don't have any point of reference on the teacher—Bingley—to know if his behavior this morning was abnormal." I drained my mug. "But I know two things. After he took off to see the chamber lady, Brigid and I agreed that he did it. Maybe 'it' will turn out to be having sex with a student instead of killing her. But he's implicated in some way."

Prager jotted a line. "What's the other thing?"

"I've known Brigid almost ten years. She might guess about someone's behavior once, twice a year—animal abuse, usually, or someone complaining about one of my city-manager decisions. She's never wrong."

"Never means she bats a thousand."

"She's never wrong."

"Easy for you to say." Prager found an empty pocket for her notebook. "She picked you to marry."

⊤

Brigid had declared chili and cornbread an unsatisfactory lunch, and Ken Bruen's latest novel incapable of holding her attention. We'd been failing a Sunday *Times* crossword puzzle when she'd told me we were going to town—to Forks—to hunt and gather.

I waited on a bench outside Windfall, the downtown thrift store, while she bargain-shopped. After observing the anemic pedestrian traffic, most of it stopping for photos beside life-size cardboard cut-outs of movie characters, I spent several minutes calculating the sales and property taxes that *Twilight* generated for the city.

A news van from one of Seattle's TV stations trolled by, and I felt a stomach burble of empathy for my Forks counterpart. Her expected week of slow pre-holiday work, or his week of Thanksgiving party preparation, had gone completely pear-shaped the instant Ashley's neck wounds got Insta'd to the universe.

"I should thank you."

I looked up from the Charles Portis novel I hadn't been reading.

Bingley, holding a steaming takeaway cup and looking shockingly bushy-tailed.

"For this morning."

"Have you—"

"The cops, yeah." He motioned at the empty space beside me, then noticed my holstered pistol. "You're a cop, too?"

"No. Your state's not reciprocal with our concealed-carry permits, but it's open-carry."

Bingley shrugged before settling himself next to me. "Prager, right? I just finished talking with her at the high school." He pointed at the building, fronted by a sign reading HOME OF THE SPARTANS.

"You got everything—"

"Out in the open." Bingley took a drink, then a long breath. "Liberating, really."

"Really."

"I told the detective that Ashley and me were—had been—" He sipped, choked, wiped his mouth with a napkin. "We'd been together since she turned eighteen. Getting married, starting a family, after she graduates next May."

"Family makes a difference at times like this."

"It could, I guess." Bingley blew out his lungs. "My wife knew—it's been over for us since before I met Ashley." He ground at his eyes with the napkin, shook his head. "We thought it would be cheaper to stay married."

Costly miscalculation.

"What else did you get out in the open?"

"I was at my mom's house last night. A raccoon came through her dog door. Her akita went psycho on it, so I was over there all night with her neighbor, cleaning up."

I thought about the stunning destructive capacity of our well-mannered dogs. "Did her dog win?"

"Tore that thing apart in two rooms." Bingley forced out a laugh. "Blood like a horror movie." Silence. "Prager called my mom. Told her they'd do some kind of test to make sure it's not human blood."

"A bunch of logistics in these things," I said. "Not like on TV."

"Prager said I hadn't broken any laws worth arresting me for, so after she checked my alibi, she said I could go." Another eye wipe. "As if there's anywhere to go. Mom's, I guess. Your mom has to take you in, right?"

More bad judgment.

"Prager tell you anything else?"

"She was calling Lizzie when I left." Sigh. "My wife. You saw her."

"In the chamber car."

Nod. "Cares more about publicity for Edward and Bella than me. Or Ashley." Another news van coasted past, the passenger rubbernecking. "The *Twilight*-themed renewal of our vows should've been my red flag. After we found out she couldn't have kids."

"I'm sorry for your losses."

Bingley sprawled on the bench, head knocking against the store window. "You and your wife were very kind to me this morning. I should thank her, too."

"She'll be a while." I wagged my book to amplify the excuse.

Bingley departed after I promised to extend his gratitude to Brigid. I took Prager's card from my pocket as he rounded the corner, tapped out the detective's number, and repeated our conversation.

"The victim—Ashley—was older," Prager said. "Missed a year of school when she was a kid after she got hit by a car. The district can fire him, but he wasn't breaking the law."

"Where does that leave you?"

"Hosed."

"Bingley and his wife had a not very pleasant conversation at the beach this morning."

"I wouldn't have a very pleasant conversation, either, if the asshole I couldn't divorce because we're broke was screwing around with a teenager."

"Did you tell him about Brigid's pregnancy guess?"

"Not until I get autopsy results. I asked Bingley if it was possible. He said no—they were careful." I visualized Prager making air quotes. "Whatever that means."

"I've seen a couple of news vans," I said.

Prager cursed.

"Can I offer you a thought?"

"I'd rather hear from your never-wrong wife."

"If you think you'll eventually charge Bingley, I'd put him on suicide watch."

"Feeling all chipper, was he?"

"Considering his circumstances." I paused as the Discover Forks SUV drove by, trailed by four news vans. "He was looking for people to thank. Used the word 'liberating.'"

Prager scribbled something. "Best idea he's had this century."

⚇

"Bingley's dead."

Prager's call came long enough past midnight that I was groggy when I answered. "How?"

"You got a bad habit of being around people who find out they're dead."

"Should I get a lawyer?"

I motioned for Brigid to go back to sleep.

"You're a lawyer," Prager said.

"Not that kind." I climbed into my clothes. "And I don't have a fool for a client, either."

That earned a humorless laugh. "If you promise not to tell my boss, I could use another set of eyes. Bounce some ideas off your thick skull." She recited an address. "The on-duty deputy over here is handling a messy car wreck, and it'll be an hour before I get my backup."

"Might take me thirty minutes to get there. Don't shoot me because I'm carrying."

"What's this I-me-mine crap? I just need you to drive the smart one over here."

⚇

Brigid spotted Prager's aging Charger before GPS told us we'd arrived. We found her walking a pattern in the side yard, flashlight extended an arm's length above her head.

Prager checked her watch. "Your sheriff told mine that you're a speed freak."

"Duty called."

Prager laughed then, warm and genuine, and pointed at her car with instructions to wait there until she finished her search.

I checked the news and read a few highlights to Brigid. Twilight Vampire Killer still won the internet. The chamber lady, Bingley's wife Lizzie, posed before various fictional landmarks in every link I tapped.

Prager opened her car's trunk, leaned in, and came out with a tablet computer. "I want the doc's opinion on the photos of his body."

Brigid looked at the house, at the crime scene tape stretched across the front door. "Is he still in there?"

"Waiting on the coroner's van." Prager displayed a photo of Bingley's face, eyes bulging and skin gone chalky. "He's in no rush."

Brigid swiped her fingers to enlarge Bingley's mouth. "Cyanotic."

"What else?"

Brigid recentered the image on the dead man's eyes. "Ashley's eyes were shut, but it looks like petechiae in his. That's probably asphyxiation."

Prager flipped to a photo of Bingley's hands. "Anything there?"

Brigid took the tablet and angled it away from the trunk's light. "That wrist has bruises like the ones I saw on Ashley's wrist."

"Same on his other wrist. Same on Ashley." Prager poked me. "What've you got, gunslinger?"

"Puncture wounds on his neck?"

"A swing and a miss. But look what I found in his pocket." She took the tablet and found an image of a block of wood with two screws drilled through it, a couple of inches apart, the sharp tips extending half an inch.

"You think you've got a serial killer?"

67

"Why would you ask that?"

"When you called, I figured he'd done himself. What sort of killer commits suicide the same way he commits murder?"

"Who says you're not the brains of this outfit?" Prager swiped the tablet until she reached a picture of a typewritten page:

I cannot live with the shame of impregnating one of the students entrusted to my care, Ashley Hagen, or of knowing the authorities eventually will find me to be her killer. "I know love and lust don't always keep the same company." In death, I beg my cherished wife's forgiveness.
Charles Bingley

I read the note twice before handing the tablet to Brigid. "Did you tell him Ashley was pregnant?"

"Nope," Prager said. "I still don't know if she was or wasn't. And he told me she couldn't—or, as far as he knew, shouldn't—be."

"We didn't say anything, either."

Brigid confirmed with a nod, distracted, reading the note.

"What else did you find to take pictures of?"

Prager opened her notebook. "Know anything about pharmaceuticals?" she said to Brigid. "The people kind?"

"The veterinary formulary has the same drugs as for people, but sometimes for different indications."

Prager put her notebook under the trunk light. "One bottle of zolpidem, scrip for thirty pills to the wife, dated eight days ago and empty."

Brigid elbowed me. "He's the insomnia expert."

"You can't overdose on those kinds of sleeping pills," I said. "But more than a couple would knock a person out."

"Like dead-to-the-world knock 'em out?"

"Even if they weren't sound asleep, they'd be too—I don't know, addled—to resist."

Prager added to her densely notated page. "I found a positive pregnancy test beside the empty pill bottle, which was beside the note."

"Bingley told me that Lizzie couldn't get pregnant," I said.

"Lizzie told me that he couldn't get her pregnant when I asked if Ashley might've been. And the test stick matches an empty box I found in Ashley Hagen's bathroom."

"What did Bingley tell you about Lizzie?"

"Not so much with the beloved," Prager said.

"Same, plus so much with the *Twilight* obsession."

Prager returned the tablet to the trunk and closed it.

"Where's Lizzie?" Brigid said.

"In the wind. She called 911 to report the body in their house. Gone when I got here."

Brigid leaned against me. "I'm sorry I said that thing about that spot on your face. But you really should have it looked at."

Prager touched it. "Is that her way of saying she's ready to go back to bed?"

I tried to remember the last time I'd heard Brigid apologize. "I think it means she likes you."

"You told me you're in town 'til early Sunday." Prager returned her notebook to one of her pockets. "I shouldn't have to bother you two again, but if it takes a couple of days to find Lizzie, I'll buy to be your third wheel at dinner."

Brigid nodded. "Any place that doesn't have one of those cardboard vampires staring at us."

⊤

I've never encountered dark like Pacific Northwest dark, blackness that swallows headlights and smothers sound. We drove thirty minutes from Forks to our cabin through a tunnel of trees in such dark. Brigid determined our best defense against it would be a fire on the beach, a warm welcome to a dawn still hours away.

She took the cabin key and went for matches and beach chairs while I took the flashlight from the car's go bag and gathered kindling. We met at the fire ring, set a small fire on the wet sand, and straddled a log to make out like teenagers while the coals got hot enough to add branches.

When I stood to fetch more wood, Brigid refused my departure. She wrapped her arms around my neck, melding her body to mine.

"You can't go," she said, "until I tell you something."

I hoisted her so we were eye to eye, her legs wrapped around my waist. "I'm all ears, Thumper."

"Poindexter, you're so much with the beloved."

"And—"

"Not like that." She raised her face to the sky. "Not like a trade. Just me, telling you. I know we're a team."

"A great—"

Brigid silenced me with an index finger on my lips. "And I know you'd be just as great without me."

"Don't—"

"Shhh. Not like a trade. You'd be *better* without me. Because I know what you do, what you give up, so I can be in polite society like a regular person." She kissed me, lightly, and then nestled her cheek on my shoulder. "Now I'm done and you can talk."

"You were amazing before I met you." *I can't function—can't sleep, can't live—without you.* "As soon as I figured it out, I asked you to marry me."

Brigid giggled, something she'd done only twice before in our years together, and neither time entirely sober. "You did what?"

"I asked—"

"You *begged*."

"Begged," I admitted.

"Three times."

"Only twice was I actually begging."

"Okay."

She bit my neck then, a nip that blasted a blue electric spike down my back and curled my toes.

"Get enough wood to last 'til sun-up." She uncurled her arms. "While you're gone, I'll come up with some ways to keep you entertained until then."

I squeezed her, lowered her, and promised I'd return as soon as humanly possible.

And when I did, I found her face-down on the beach, blood flowing black from her head.

The chamber lady, Bingley's wife Lizzie, squatted on my wife's back and held a huge kitchen knife at her neck.

I cried Brigid's name as time solidified in my heart, as I watched for the rise and fall of Brigid's chest.

"Stay there," Lizzie said.

"Sure." I saw Brigid breathing and unclenched my guts. "Whatever you want."

"She told the cops that Ashley was having my baby."

"My arms are tired. Can I put this wood down?"

"No." She squeezed her eyes shut for a second. "I don't care. Yes. Just stay there."

I angled the hip with my holster away from the fire. I couldn't see Brigid's pistol. "I'm going to crouch, so I can drop this wood without smashing my feet." *If Lizzie found Brigid's gun, why the knife?*

"Just remember." Lizzie pressed the knife against Brigid's skin, making a crease.

I bent my knees, my holster now opposite the fire, and dropped the wood. In its clattering fall, I straightened and drew my pistol without having to worry that she'd hear the holster snap.

Clear line of fire.

I kept my gun arm, my left arm, snug against my body, pistol hidden by my thigh.

Nothing behind Lizzie.

"Boy," I said. "You've really been all over the news."

dbschlosser

"You've seen my clippings?"

"You're nationwide."

If I miss, the sound and sight of gunfire will scare her off Brigid before she can do any real damage with the knife.

"Global, I'll bet."

Unless she hits the carotid.

"The bite wound was—well, it was inspired."

"The vampire thing was easy—just a belt around their wrists and a dry cleaner bag until they stopped." A shiver passed through Lizzie then, visibly, like a dog shaking off water. "Out here on tribal land, you two should be killed by werewolves."

For the first time, I regretted not reading far enough in the novels to know what that implied.

"That'll dominate the whole news cycle," I said. "You'll have Forks on every TV in the world."

"If more people read our books, I'll finally start boosting our off-season occupancy rates."

"I wonder if killing a couple of tourists might not be your best strategy."

She jerked her head, then squinted at me. "Werewolves have always been the enemies of vampires."

Another swing and a miss. "You have an occupancy tax yet, Elizabella? That could really pump up your advertising spend." *Should've at least watched the movies.* "Can I call you Elizabella?"

Lizzie grew half a smile.

She seemed so mesmerized by her nickname that I almost felt bad when I shot her.

☂

"I'm getting sick of your faces."

Prager closed her notebook and traded Brigid a fresh cold pack for the one that my wife held over her bandaged head wound. "His, anyway."

Brigid gave me a sideways glance from the back bumper of the ambulance. "I was pretty glad to see it. So glad, I saw two of it."

"That's your concussion talking." Prager offered a Hydro Flask of steaming coffee. "You'll be back to suffering only one of him in no time."

Brigid waved off the drink. "Caffeine is associated with bad neurological outcomes after concussion."

"I keep forgetting you're a doctor."

"My lawyer will keep reminding you."

Prager told Brigid she needed a word with her lawyer. She waited until Brigid acknowledged her, then ushered me toward her car. "Nice shooting, cowboy."

"I was aiming for her vital T."

"Shoulder was off by a foot or so." Prager scratched her nose. "What's a nice boy like you know about the vital T?"

"My baby brother's a Marine. When he's home, we bet on who can blow out the most on pictures of foreign dictators."

"Why don't we keep that between you and me." Prager searched some of her pockets for nothing she found. "The chamber lady tell you anything else that you want just between you and me?"

"I gave you the whole truth and nothing but. I think she figured that as long as she'd killed her husband's pregnant mistress, she might as well use the body to improve her PR metrics."

"You're a very interesting civilian, Parker Glynn." Prager nodded into the dawn sky. "After that thing back where you're from, this might start to earn you something of a reputation."

"You know what they say." I took Prager's Hydro Flask and a long swallow of bitter coffee. "No PR is bad PR."

ʈʈʈ

73

THE GRENADE
Roz Ray

Dear Hammett,
   I didn't write like I said I would. I'm writing now, but it's not what you've been expecting. If you're getting this letter, it means I've done something stupid, and I need your help. San Francisco may be a long ways away, but then again it might be just far enough for you to do what I need done. And if you can't, or you don't, or you say *forget it Josie I'm through*—I guess I probably won't be around to notice.

I'm a good nurse. A great nurse, maybe the best, but I'm about as lousy a detective as you can get. You told me once, I don't know if you remember, but you told me your rules for detective work:
   Don't get involved
   Don't get noticed
   Don't get impatient
   Thing is, I'm impatient by nature, I'm up to my ears in I-don't-know-what, and if I get noticed, well, that's where you come in.

I don't know how all the pieces fit together yet, and when I do, maybe I'll burn this letter and you'll never have to read it. Until then, I can tell you it started with Phil Sanders and Little Ronnie Rooney. Well, it started long before that.

There was a down day, a little while before you were discharged. The whole ward was quiet, so you and me were swapping war stories. You were telling me about driving ambulances, and I was telling you about working in the casualty clearing stations, and how often I was put on triage. I could always tell who was going to make it and who wasn't. Who was worth the doctor's time, and who was just stealing time away from the next guy. You asked me why the boys never let me play cards with them, when all the other nurses have a standing invitation. Turns out, if you're good at reading people up to your hips in mud and blood, you'll be even better at reading them in a bright white sanitarium wing in rainy Tacoma, Washington. My point is: I can always tell who's gonna win and who's gonna lose, who's gonna live and who's gonna die, and Phil Sanders and Little Ronnie Rooney should have lived.

But they didn't.

Phil and Ronnie came in with pneumonia, like you, and they were getting better, like you. Until, well, the doc called it death due to respiratory complications. Natural causes. Which I would have bought, except that there wasn't anything natural about it.

I checked everything. Prescriptions, dosages, meals. I didn't know what I was looking for, but I checked every linen closet, supply closet, the bedrooms, the attic, the office, the foyer, and eventually, the basement.

For all my time near the front lines, barely a cannon-shot away from the trenches, you'd think I'd've seen the worst of humanity, and I'd've said you were right. That would be a mistake. It turns out my biggest mistake, my worst flaw as a detective thus far? Lack of imagination. That wasn't on your list, by the way, so you'll pardon me for not taking it into account. If you had bet me that someone would open up a bootlegging operation in a sleepy little hospital like Cushman, I might have laid down fifty-fifty odds. If you bet me that that same someone would start testing their moonshine on the patients? I would've laughed you straight out of the building.

But that's what they're doing. At least, I *think* that's what they're doing.

I found a still in the basement, empty jugs of industrial alcohol in a pile next to it. I think somebody's playing chemist, trying to turn denatured alcohol into the kind of alcohol you drink, instead of the kind of alcohol that'll kill you. They must've slipped Ronnie and Phil a dose of moonshine in place of cough medicine, before they'd gotten their formula quite right. And who knows if they *have* gotten their formula right. Maybe more of our boys are about to die...

...I think I've blundered my way through this thing pretty much as you'd expect. Where you would've been patient, where you would've gathered clues on the sly, where you never would've let on that you were *on* to anything out of the ordinary, I...*didn't* do any of those things.

I'm sure someone saw me go down to the basement, and I'm sure someone knows what I'd find when I got there. The question is: who knows, and how many of them are there?

There's a certain genius to testing this stuff out on respiratory patients, though, isn't there. TB is a capricious bastard, mustard gas poisoning is a waking nightmare, pneumonia gets house odds at best, and the layman might never know who would be up and who would be down, who would walk out the front door, and who would get wheeled out the back.

But I knew. I've always known.

I've been meaning to write you a letter for so long. Not this letter. A different letter. A *proper* letter. The kind of letter...the kind of letter a man might like to read from a lady some sunny afternoon in San Francisco.

Those afternoons you helped me around the ward, folding sheets...your straight-up-and-downness, even when you could barely lift your head off your chest. Your damnable *manners*. You really get under my skin, you know that? In my life, I've never felt compelled to impress anyone the way I do with you, and I wonder, if I'd never met you, would I have done any of this? Would I have counted Ronnie and Phil as a miscalculation, and gone no further? Doesn't matter much now, I guess.

One of two things might happen after I finish this letter: whoever poisoned Ronnie and Phil will find out that I know about the still and come after me, or, if by some miracle I figure out who it is before they sniff me out, I'll tell the chief of police about it on my way out of town. If it's the latter, you'll likely never see this letter, because I won't have to send it. If it's the former, then hopefully I have time to get this in the mail before anything happens.

The boys brought in a German once, not too long before Armistice. They'd found him in an artillery crater, thigh-shot, dry-heaving from the pain. He had a map case with him, which they wanted, and he knew they wanted it. They'd've shot him in the head from twenty paces to get that map case, except that he'd pulled the pin out of a grenade, and was holding it up in his bloody hand. If they left him in the crater, he'd've blown himself up and the map case with him. If they shot him, he'd've dropped the grenade and blown himself up and the map case with him. They couldn't ignore him, and they couldn't kill him, so they brought him in.

I don't know what happened to him after we sewed up his leg, but I'll tell you this: whoever built that still in the basement is not going to ignore me, and I don't want to die. So you're my grenade. I'm hoping you are, anyway. I want to be able to tell whoever follows me into a shadowy alley one day that there's a detective in San Francisco who knows everything I know, and that if he doesn't hear from me on the regular, he'll expose the whole operation. Hopefully that buys me enough time to get out of here. Hopefully, on the heels of this letter, you get another letter, a nicer letter, from some far off place with big skies. And if that letter never comes, I want you to know that it's not because I didn't want to write it.

Yours, always,
Josie

🍄🍄🍄

RESTORATION SOFTWARE
Robert J. Binney

T he lock didn't even require picking. Fact is, most locks are installed wrong to begin with. Then you add years of drunks and pros and johns and wife-beaters and beaten wives slamming the door, plus a nonexistent maintenance staff, and even a moron with a pocketknife could jimmy his way in.

And make no mistake, the two rain-soaked thugs breaking in were morons.

Traffic raced past, headlights barely glancing off the intruders. Used to be that Aurora Avenue, the too-narrow three-lane escape route from downtown Seattle, was littered with places like this—"no-tell" motels rented by either the hour or the month. It wasn't always random indiscretions behind these mostly hollow doors; cops, teachers, and newly divorced department store managers were all just as likely to need a temporary bed as some runaway. In the weeks before Alaska king crab season, and crews steaming out the Ballard Locks, you couldn't get a room at any price.

But these days, the Stay-Rite, broadcasting its Free HBO and Microwave Oven in neon, was the last of a dying breed. First Microsoft money and now Amazon money crept through downtown and then Belltown, razing local history for fancy reclaimed-materials towers in retro colors that robbed this once-rugged logging town of its soul.

"You gonna bitch? Or you gonna work?"

Jonah, the older of the two, stepped inside and lit his arm-length Maglite, weighed down by D cells; his partner used the flashlight app on his iPhone. A goddamn app! Good luck swinging that in a fight.

"Just saying, I kinda miss the old days. You could earn decent and get a place near the water."

"Whaddaya mean, 'the old days'? I got flannel shirts older than you."

"So do I. Buy 'em at Pioneer Thrift."

It didn't take much effort for the two of them to toss the place. A one-room "efficiency," the bedroom was the living room was the kitchen. Everything had the slightly mildewy smell of fleece that had been worn and put away damp, over and over again.

A mostly-empty growler—its remnants hazy, hints of mango fighting the hops—attracted fruit flies on the counter. The bed, unmade, showed signs of a single sleeper. No hanky-panky. The older thug opened and closed dresser drawers while his companion rifled through the closet, the rings of the anti-theft hangers like the brake pads on his brother-in-law's El Camino.

"Get the feeling we're being watched?"

"That's just nerves."

This was Jonah's favorite part of the job, rooting through strange women's things. Particularly their privates. When his partner—he thought his name was Grant, or Gus, he never bothered learning with the new kids but there was something tattooed on his neck—wasn't looking, he'd take a sniff. They were under strict "Leave No Trace" orders, so he couldn't take any souvenirs. But one pink pair of hip-huggers caught his eye. They looked like they might fit, and his pulse raced, just thinking about how the silky polyester would feel.

"Whoa...Shit! Gnarly!"

Gus—or Grant—came out of the bathroom, a palmful of hair dripping on the chipped tile. The long strands, a bushy, tangled mess, spilled in all directions. "It's...sticky. Like pine tar or something."

Jonah grunted and wondered why he even picked it up. "Not hers. You saw the pictures. Short, straight hair. Blonde. Not...what is that? Looks like the carpet in my basement."

"She coulda cut it and dyed it. And that's why it's here."

Kid had a point.

"Weird it was just on the floor, like not in the drain or anything." He flicked it back where he found it, the gloppy pile smacking against the floor. "Find anything?"

Jonah shook his head and closed the drawers, carefully smoothing the nightgowns into place while his partner slid the closet shut, his phone's flashlight bouncing off the mirrored door.

In the mirror, thin, beady red eyes danced behind him.

"Shit! Oh shit! Shit! Shitshitshit!"

He fumbled his phone, dropped it, firing its beam on the ceiling.

"Hell you on about?" Jonah spun his beam right into his partner's eyes.

"I saw something. It...was looking at me."

"The woman's here?"

"It was an 'it.' And it moved."

Jonah painted the room with his Maglite. He didn't see anything. The curtain fluttering in the open door's draft was the only movement. He walked to where Gus had been standing and slid the closet door back and forth. He thought he saw a shadow, but more likely it was the light ricocheting off the folding mirrors, like the cover of that Pink Floyd CD.

"Its eyes were on fire."

"Look, it's the goddamned Exit sign." Sure enough, the light from outside blinked on and off, right at eye level, in the mirror. "Now go put the bathroom back together. Make sure her powders and makeup and shit looks right."

Jonah kneeled to pick up the kid's phone. He heard a slapping sound behind him—reminded him of his swim coach

81

sneaking up on him after practice—and he spun his light. Nothing.

The two thugs took one last look around and made for the door. On the white tiles the Maglite caught a muddy footprint. Not a shoe print, but a bare foot. And not the dainty arch of the woman they were pursuing, this stretched across several tiles. At least one-and-a-half times bigger than Jonah's size 14 boot.

"Do you...think that's..."

Jonah snapped off his light and lightly slapped the back of his partner's head. "That's just your imagination, kid. There ain't no such thing as—"

☂

"You Sasquatch?"

"What it says on the door."

In fact, it didn't. The WeWork rules strictly prohibit tenants from installing any personal signage. Some nonsense about aesthetics. That didn't stop them from charging fifty bucks a month for a shingle behind the receptionist. He just liked saying that; he heard it on a detective show once and thought it sounded cool.

The line had one of two effects on dames. It either slaps what little self-confidence they have left right out of their mugs, and they wobble on their heels into the chair opposite the bigfooted detective's desk, hands nervously clutching their pocketbook on their laps...or this. This one oh-so-subtly raised her freshly tweezed eyebrows, pursed her lips, tucked back her long raven hair, and took command of her strut across the office.

She crossed her yoga-toned legs. It took all his effort not to check if she was Sharon Stone-ing him. She used her pinky nail to pick an imaginary speck off the corner of those lips. Trying to unnerve him. Wouldn't work.

Sasquatch, Private Investigator, had been leaning back in his chair. He wanted to look like he was thinking deeply about a case, but he was having more fun seeing just how far he could tilt. If he balanced just right, it made his tummy feel funny and he pretended he was flying.

But now that he had a client, Sasquatch had to look serious. He came forward, too fast, and the wheels skidded out from under him. His arms spun at his sides as he fumbled to steady himself. He grabbed the desk and hoped it looked natural. Furniture was still a strange concept, and he wasn't really that good at chairs. He'd much prefer to pop a squat on a rotten log, but the others in his suite complained about the grubs.

He shuffled some papers on his desk. He didn't know what any of them were—he couldn't read—but he'd seen the move on a different show and thought it looked professional.

"You are...?"

"Marilyn Kegel. I have an appointment."

"We finally meet in person."

She wrinkled her nose.

"Do you have a dog?"

"What? No. Look, I did what you asked on the telephone. I went to your motel room—"

"Did anyone see you?"

"Why are you so nervous, Miss Kegel?"

She smoothed her pencil-thin skirt.

"I...I'm not nervous."

Sasquatch shook his head. "You can cover it up with perfume, but I can smell it."

"Did you find the documents?"

"Why did you lie to me about whose room it was?"

She came around to his side of the desk, picked a burr off his chest. Played with the gold chain around his neck. He might be an eight-foot-tall mythological savage covered in mottled, tangled fur, but he was no dummy.

"Why won't you answer my questions?"

"Not until you answer mine." He swatted her hand away.

"Whose room?"

Marilyn bit her lip flirtatiously. "What makes you think it wasn't mine? That I invited you up for a little tête-à-tête?"

"A couple of reasons. Chief being, the clothing in there was all size twelve or fourteen. And you are...not." Also, he didn't know what a tête-à-tête even was. "So whose room?"

He could hear her lipstick crinkle.

"It was my sister's room. But you knew that."

"Of course." He had had no idea.

"I guess you have to be smart, to make up for..." She waved her hand, dismissively.

He shrugged. *What?*

"I mean, don't detectives have to be sneaky? To skulk about and lurk?"

"What makes you think I can't be stealthy?"

"You're so...big."

He chuckled. It came out husky, like a cougar's growl.

"I'm pretty good at being elusive."

His guest looked skeptical.

"Go ahead, try to take my picture."

She started to protest but leaned back on the desk. In the time it took her to pick up her phone and open the camera, he was gone. Marilyn gasped and looked around the room.

Sasquatch stepped out from the room's corner, where'd he'd disappeared in the shadows.

"Now why don't you tell me what this is really about. You told me there'd be folders of documents in that room. I thoroughly searched, and there was no paperwork of any kind."

She took a deep breath and made her eyes grow big, he supposed in an attempt to look frightened. "Her ex-husband had been threatening her, so she stole those documents—"

He held up his hand to stop her. "And you need them, why?"

"She's missing, don't you see? And now this! Please help me!" Again, she threw herself at him, burying her fake tears in his shaggy chest.

He couldn't deny that it felt nice. But he wasn't going to fall for another client, not after last time. He pushed her away and loped back toward his desk.

Dejected, she fumbled through her purse for a cigarette and flicked her lighter. His paw snapped out and stopped her.

She rolled her eyes in frustration and muttered something about the nanny state.

He held tight. "What about secondhand smoke? Cancer? Forest fires?"

"*Forest fires*? I thought that was the other guy's thing. With the hat."

"Forest fires are bad for everyone." He sniffed the air and nodded behind her. "Seems like cities aren't much safer. The two goons that rolled your sister's motel room are paying a visit."

They heard a commotion in the kombucha lounge outside his door, and through the frosted-glass walls he made out the shadows of panicked suitemates running away. So many goddamn glass walls at WeWork. He opened his desk drawer and pulled out his .357 just as Jonah and Gus kicked his door in.

The smart play would be to breach in a two-man hatch-and-flank, one low and the other high; these were not smart men. After fighting with the weight of the door, they bumped against each other and fired blindly into the office.

Sasquatch realized he was never going to get his furniture deposit back.

He grabbed Marilyn's wrist and pulled him behind her.

"Put your arms around my neck," he barked.

She did as told.

Taking one step backward, he kicked at the glass panel. It gave way and shattered into the architect's office next door. A man in floodwater slacks and a bowtie yelped.

"Sorry, Mitch," Sasquatch said. "Kicked the wrong one."

He used his other foot to press on a neighboring pane. It popped out and crashed to the ground, four stories below.

"Hold on," he told Marilyn, and he leaned out of the breach and grabbed the gutter pipe, hoping it would hold their weight.

☂

They huddled between dumpsters in the alley. If this was one of those days when SPD swept Third Avenue clean, every nook and cranny back here would be filled with addicts smoking out of tin foil, or toothless schizophrenics shitting through the flaps of makeshift tents.

Sasquatch tried to have empathy for them; he knew what it was like to be ridden roughshod out of your home and trapped away from your element, even as he was disgusted by the litter and animal-like suffering on the streets. He didn't know what the answer was, but he knew it wasn't this.

Luckily, today wasn't one of those days. The prolonged rain had hosed things down, so only the faint smell of piss lingered among Wild Ginger's trash bags. He pulled Marilyn close, deeper into the shadows, as Gus and Jonah splashed by, oblivious. Seattleites loved bitching about mid-afternoon twilight, but it had its advantages.

He could tell Marilyn was terrified. Whatever she thought she was getting into, she hadn't bargained for gunshots and jumping out of windows. He felt her heart racing while she tried to catch her breath. He stroked her hair to calm her.

Her hands snaked up around his neck. Her breathing slowed, falling into sync with his. She looked up at him. In his eyes. Beauty to beast.

Ever the coquette, she pulled up onto her tiptoes and whispered, "You saved my life."

Sasquatch took her hand. "Your brother-in-law's men?"

"Hm?"

He nodded up the alley. "Your sister's husband. The woman we're saving."

"Right."

"So who is this guy?"

"I thought you knew."

"Of course I know," he lied. "But I want to hear it from you."

She nuzzled his neck. "Cameron Blacksmith."

Sasquatch was both impressed and intimidated.

Cameron Blacksmith was one of the first dot-com millionaires in the '90s, and he'd only grown richer and more powerful. He and one or two others owned most of Seattle's real estate, and its sports teams, and all of its industry. A guy with power like that left few places for Marilyn's sister to hide. Or Marilyn, for that matter.

Sasquatch took one look to his right at the disappearing goons, pulled her into the alley and ran to the left. She stopped, digging in like a stubborn puppy. "Don't you find me attractive?"

He did not. Too bony and lanky. He knew enough about women, though, to let her down easy. "Look, Ms. Kegel. It's not you. It's...it's not even mating season."

"There they are!"

Behind Sasquatch and Marilyn, Jonah yelled to his partner. They turned and ran back toward the fleeing detective and his distressed damsel.

Sasquatch grabbed her wrist and ran out onto the side street, stopping in front of his Buick Riviera. He pulled the passenger door open.

"Get in!"

"What the hell is this?" She looked more terrified of his car than of the gunmen. "There's no roof!"

"It's a T-top! I need the headroom!"

"It's pouring rain!"

An errant pistol shot ricocheted at their feet.

"It's about to rain bullets, sweetheart!"

One sniff of the coupe's mildewed interior and she shook free from his grip, running across the street toward two Lime scooters. A passerby yelled at her for jaywalking as more shots rang out. Sasquatch ran after her, and the passerby threatened to call the cops on both of them.

"I can't ride one of these," he said.

She had already swiped her phone over one scooter, causing it to light up and unlock, and she started to do the same on the other. "Don't worry, I'm paying."

"You don't understand. I *can't* !"

"Nonsense! It's so easy!" Marilyn stood and kicked away, racing down the sidewalk toward the waterfront and narrowly missing pedestrians.

Groaning, Sasquatch put one foot on his scooter and its deck collapsed under his weight.

He stepped backward, disappearing into the shadows, while Jonah and Gus ran past.

☂

Sasquatch still had not heard from Marilyn by the next afternoon. He supposed he should put some effort into finding her, but she wasn't his primary client, after all. Even if she didn't know that.

Besides, he was hungry.

He strolled along Pike Place Market, pushing past The Line. Even in the rain, there was always The Line. Idiots waiting an hour for a cup of coffee. He had given up yelling at people that it wasn't the "original shop"; the corporate website said it was, so that's that. *It's amazing, the crazy nonsense people believe on the internet*, Sasquatch thought.

His stomach growled. Most people went to Ivar's or Elliott's for takeout, but to his way of thinking, there was nothing better than catching a fresh salmon in his teeth.

As if on cue, the Market fishmonger yelled out, "Hey, Chewie!" and tossed a ten-pound Coho over the crowd.

Sasquatch laughed. "No autographs!" he shouted, and took a bite out of the fish, like an apple. If he'd known that would be the last pleasant moment of his day, he would have savored it.

Before he finished his lunch, his keen rainforest hearing detected a familiar sound—Marilyn Kegel, screaming. He ran to the top of the Hill Climb and scanned the area.

There! He saw the backs of the previous night's goons down at the Seattle Aquarium's otter exhibit.

His big feet took the steps three, four at a time, and he ran through the waterfront construction to save her. But he was too late.

☂

Sasquatch leaned against the side of the Seattle Aquarium, more upset than he should have been, watching the medics fish Marilyn's floating body out of the tank.

Even with all the commotion—emergency workers, press, lookie-loos—no one gave the towering furball a second glance.

No one, that is, except for Inspector Ness, somehow always first on the scene. They made quite a pair to anyone paying attention—five-and-a-half feet in work boots and receding gray curls, he had to crane his neck to speak to Sasquatch. He grilled the private detective about another dead client, and confiscated his weapon.

Sasquatch tried to protest—Marilyn hadn't even been shot— and he'd almost convinced the inspector when he saw, across the pier, his chief suspect: Cameron Blacksmith. He excused himself and lumbered after him.

☂

If Cameron Blacksmith thought he could shake a giant feral bipedal hominid who was also a licensed private investigator, he had another think coming, Sasquatch thought, laughing to himself.

Blacksmith slinked into the crowd queued up at the Great Wheel, but the Bigfoot caught up to him just as he paid his admission and boarded a private gondola.

Sasquatch strolled past the ticket taker and climbed in with the elusive entrepreneur. "Surprised?"

"Of course not. I knew you'd follow me here."

Blacksmith grabbed a handful of trail mix, popped it in his mouth, and offered the bag to his new companion.

Sasquatch shook his head. He'd eaten enough nuts and berries to last a lifetime. "You're less lumpy than you look in the paper."

Blacksmith threw back his bald head and cackled.

"After my divorce, I got buff. You don't land a smokeshow like Marilyn without burning a few calories. You know, I could hook you up. A little Paleo, some wax…You'd be something!"

Sasquatch looked out the window, fogging it, amazed at how quickly the streetscape recovered from a murder scene to a tourist thoroughfare.

"Not going to offer your condolences, detective? I have very recently become widowed."

"Marilyn was your second wife," Sasquatch muttered.

Blacksmith nodded.

"I knew that." He had not. "So what's your game, Mr. Blacksmith? What is everybody going crazy for?"

The Ferris wheel groaned under the unexpected bulk of its newest passenger as it started its rotation.

"Control, Mr. Sasquatch. Control."

"How do these documents give you control?"

"They're not just documents! I knew I shouldn't have expected a stupid ape to understand true genius!"

Sasquatch bristled, hoping Blacksmith didn't notice that the man was getting under his fur. "It's more like an app?"

That laugh again. An actual supervillain's cackle. "No, not

an app! But complete control. Forget the One Seattle Plan—I'm talking about making the parks safe again, air and water clean, every day a sunny day..."

"That actually sounds great. How does your app do that?"

Blacksmith sighed. "Not an app. First, I take the parks— Myrtle Edwards, Discovery, Gas Works, even that shitty small one—and transfer their deeds to me."

"Privatize them."

"You do get it! Build luxury condos and get rid of the riff-raff, the drugs, the filth, the protesters..."

"Get rid of them? Where will they go?"

"Tacoma?" he scoffed. "What? You think they'll notice the smell?"

This wasn't sounding as terrible as it should, Sasquatch felt. But, still. "Don't you see how guys like you are the reason..." He realized this was futile and changed tacks. "How will you stop the rain? Clear the air?"

"You know the roof on the ballpark?"

"You're going to put a roof over the city?"

Blacksmith tapped his forefinger on Sasquatch's forehead and nodded. He sat back and shoved more trail mix into his smug kisser.

Maybe not a terrible idea, but certainly a crazy one. "What's in it for you?"

Blacksmith was already leaning forward; the carriage was tilted heavily toward Sasquatch's side. He pulled himself closer to his companion and held his gaze. "Think."

Sasquatch did. He thought hard. Finally it dawned on him. "You're going to sell advertising on the inside of the dome?"

The tech billionaire slapped his knee, barely containing his glee.

"You'll also control the air that people breathe. And the water that they can drink. Which means you can add—"

"Nutrients. Vitamins. People will be the healthiest they've ever been!"

"I was going to say 'poison', but..." Sasquatch watched the city rising on his horizon and tried to picture anything good coming out of this plan. He couldn't. Then he noticed the gun Blacksmith was pointing at him. "I've seen this movie. I think I even streamed it on your service. You're no Orson Welles, sir."

Blacksmith smirked. "Why don't you just give me that chain that's around your neck."

"You know I can't do tha—" Sasquatch sniffed the air. "Have you been shooting pool?"

"What?"

He had suddenly picked up the smell of talcum powder. Even as the detective realized what was about to happen, he was too slow to stop it.

Glass erupted throughout the gondola. Sasquatch instinctive-ly hugged himself, hoping to protect his vitals from the gunshot. He didn't feel a thing. Confused, he looked up and saw the red stain expanding across Blacksmith's chest.

The visionary slumped in his seat, spilling his gorp, and fell forward against the doors, fading fast.

Sasquatch mumbled, "All this death and suffering, over an app."

Blacksmith reached out to grab Sasquatch's hairy arm. It was as close a connection to humanity as either had had in a while. Blood bubbled up over his lips.

"It's...not...an...app" were the last words of the planet's sixth-wealthiest man.

➇

The poor teenager working the ride had no idea what to do with a dead gunshot victim, and Sasquatch didn't care. He stepped his hairy legs over the body and onto the pier. He knew he had only minutes before Ness showed up, trying to pin the murder on him.

Joke's on the inspector, Sasquatch thought. He already confiscated my weapon.

He trudged to the parking deck, where the two thugs were leaning against his Buick. "Careful you don't scratch the finish, boys." As if another mark on its dented, rusty finish would even be noticed.

They didn't budge.

"Look, guys, your boss is dead. No need to keep hounding me."

"We had nothing to do with that," the older one, Jonah, said.

"I know." Sasquatch actually did know that. "If you get to the house before the cops do, you can have your own private estate sale, pick up a few nice things, if you know what I mean?" He nudged Jonah conspiratorially, causing the big thug to turn red.

His partner—the one with the neck tattoo—tried to look tough.

How does anyone forget to not get their neck tattooed, Sasquatch wondered.

"We just was wondering where all the paperwork was stashed in that motel room, and how's you sneaked it past us and all."

Sasquatch pushed them both aside and opened his car door.

"You never heard of DocuSign? C'mon, boys, it's all about the apps."

T

After a case, Sasquatch liked to clear his head by hitting the open road and blasting some tunes. Pulling out of the garage, he still didn't have closure on this one. He shook the water out of his Foghat eight-track tape and popped it in the dash and tried to peel out.

Traffic wasn't on his side today. Closed lanes, poorly timed lights, mostly empty buses crowding intersections. "Slow Ride," indeed. He squished in his rain-sopped seat and groaned.

He needed some time to himself, and yesterday's hijinks had earned him a permanent ban at WeWork. He made a U-turn across First—"Fuckin Uber!" someone yelled at him—and pointed the Riviera toward Eastlake.

☂

The climbing wall at the outfitter's flagship store essentially became a storage rack for returns during the pandemic and never reopened. That made it perfect for Sasquatch, since it meant no belayed eight-year-olds grinding their Amy's Organic crumbs into the handholds while he tried to think.

No one saw him as he scaled to the top. This was his favorite place in the city to reflect. Stretched out, in the glass-ceilinged atrium with fake plants and water sounds, Sasquatch started to empathize with Blacksmith's plan.

He wasn't sure how long he'd been there—it had been dark outside for a while—before he smelled her baby powder.

It took a few minutes of huffing and puffing, but eventually the first ex-Mrs. Cameron Blacksmith pulled herself to the top of the wall to join Sasquatch.

"Hello, Ms. Astor."

"Constance, please."

He lifted the gold chain from around his neck and handed her the tiny thumb drive that had been dangling from it.

"You were right, Constance, people lost their minds looking for this."

"Thank you for 'stealing' it from my motel room. I didn't know what they'd do to me if they found me. Or this. And the gall of that whore to hire you!"

"She told me you were sisters."

"Do we look anything alike?"

His eyes lingered over her body longer than professionally necessary. No, she was the opposite of Marilyn Kegel in many ways. *Niña pera*, the guys working the logging trucks would have called her. He would have liked spending time plucking that pear.

But one thing still nagged at him.

"Did you have to kill him?"

"He had to be stopped."

Sasquatch said he was confident that the city's crushing bureaucracy—the "Seattle Process"—would have moved with typically sluglike speeds and ground her ex-husband's plans to dust before the first permit was issued.

"But I couldn't take that chance. 'Money talks' and all that."

"So you stopped him." He nodded at the USB stick. "And now you have the app."

"It's more than an app! It's a revolution!"

Uh-oh, Sasquatch thought. *Here we go again.*

"You don't understand!" She turned and grabbed his paws. "With this I can roll everything back! Join me!"

"Roll what back?" He lay down, counting water spots in the acoustic tile.

"This is *control*! Don't you see that, you big lug? We can shut down the grid. Power. Internet. Sewers. Light rail."

"Losing all that will piss people off. They won't notice the light rail, but everything else."

"That's the point! They'll leave! Didn't you see the bunnies return when we locked everything down? Imagine that at scale. Everyone leaves, the buildings crumble, and nature returns! We will create a New Eden! Right here! Think about it!"

That was the second time today he'd been told to think. A New Eden did sound wonderful. But even as he entertained the idea of returning to the woods, he knew it was already too late. Too late for Seattle, too late for him, and definitely too late for Constance Astor.

Sasquatch leaned over the wall and extended his paw to Inspector Ness, tangled in his climbing harness, ears sticking out of a too-large helmet he grabbed off a mannequin.

Propping himself on one elbow, the inspector winked at Sasquatch. "You never make it easy for me, do you?" He shifted awkwardly and flashed his badge at Constance. "And you're under arrest."

Constance slapped Sasquatch. "I thought we had something!"

"I did too. But you murdered two people. And I got kicked out of my office." He grabbed the sexiest woman he'd ever met and threw her over his shoulder.

Her fists pounding against his back, Sasquatch scaled down the wall, taking her to the police car idling in the parking lot.

☂☂☂

A DOG'S YEAR
Tod Goldberg

California was a done deal for me. Didn't even bother to tell my sister or mother, figuring that when the time came, I'd get back with them and we'd sort out who owed what to who. That's the nice thing about family. They don't usually hunt you down over bad debts. I ended up in Klamath Falls working for my ex-cousin-in-law Dale, who ran the night shift at the Purple Flamingo Casino, which wasn't really a casino in the conventional sense back then, but just a bar with six video poker machines, plus Keno and Tuesday night karaoke, and then a fairly active meth and girl business in the parking lot. This was back in 2001, when having video poker was still relatively new and exciting and people hadn't started to lose their houses from it. The place was owned by the Gabarian brothers, Fred and Rodney, who were twins, but didn't look all that much alike since Rodney had a cleft palate as a kid, but who Dale claimed were connected to some organized shit up in Canada, but I didn't buy it. For one, they drove Subarus. No one in a Subaru was ever connected to shit.

Dale had me working the grill, which I was good at, and for the first month, I thought maybe I could spend some time in Klamath Falls. Maybe I'd get some cash together and buy a trailer over at the Casablanca Trailer Estates, which had its own bowling alley and eighteen-hole golf course, according to the

97

flyer pinned up in the break room. Maybe I'd get fat and comfortable and cotton to small-town Oregon living, get used to the militia fucks I saw at the grocery store strutting around like they were somebody because they wore their guns on the outside of their clothes.

The thing about *maybe* is it has a lot of off-ramps between *may* and *be*.

Because the next week Dale asked me if I could help him out with a small favor and of course I said yes, even before I knew what the favor might entail. Dale was kind of dogshit, but he'd put me on the payroll at the Purple, was letting me sleep on his Murphy bed rent-free, and for a little while he'd been family. Whatever that means.

He brought me into his office, which was surprisingly spacious. There was a big desk that Dale shared with the other assistant managers, a mini-fridge, a sunken caramel-colored leather sofa that had the imprint of every ass that had ever sat on it, and a broken jukebox filled with old 45s from the '80s. It played only "Jessie's Girl" now, so if you liked Rick Springfield, you were in luck. There was a window that looked out to the parking lot and the street beyond. It was raining outside, like every other night in Klamath Falls, so the pavement glowed a dreamy purple from the neon lights out front.

"Close the door," Dale said. He sat down behind the desk, lit up a cigarette, even though we were a non-smoking establishment, and motioned for me to sit also.

"If I sit," I told him, "I'll fall asleep." It was one in the morning. I'd been on my feet all night. There'd been a softball tournament at the junior college down the street and the winning team had come in at nine and were still out there, drinking, eating burgers, and losing money on our rigged machines. PJ, our waitress, was off and so it was just me and Dale running drinks and food all night.

"I need to open the safe," he said, "and I'm not comfortable with you watching me do it."

"I don't do that shit anymore."

"Since when?"

"My eyesight isn't that good," I said. "You don't meet a lot of safecrackers with shitty eyes."

"Since when?" he asked again.

"Turning forty-five," I said. "Everything looks like it's underwater now."

"Humor me," he said. He pointed at the couch.

"Fine," I said. I sat down and closed my eyes, to really sell it. I heard Dale's chair creak, heard the spinning of the combination, counted the seconds...figured the combo was something like 17, 33, 9. You break into enough cheap safes (and this *was* a cheap safe; they had a full vault in the basement that Dale didn't have access to, which was smart; Dale not even being an ex-con like me, but an actual working con), you never forget precisely how long it should take to get to every number. It wasn't about the eyes, not really, it was about the ears and your fingertips and dumb luck. Anyway. I was serious about that shit. If I was going to rip a safe, it certainly wasn't going to be the Purple Flamingo's safe. I didn't believe the Gabarians were connected, but I had the good sense to know they weren't a bunch of priests, either, considering everyone on the payroll got paid in cash.

I heard the safe open—the hinges could use some WD-40—and then Dale slapped something on his desk, shut the door, spun the combination, got up, came across the room, sat down next to me, a manila envelope on his lap.

"You can open your fucking eyes," Dale said. "Anyone looking for you in Seattle?"

"Last time I was there," I said, "I went to the Space Needle with your ex-wife."

"Why?"

"I don't really know," I said.

This was back when my mother was living with that cult down by Pasco and I was staying with my Uncle Aaron in

Oakland. He was always driving back and forth to Canada to get weed and he'd take us with him for the fifteen-hour drive to Vancouver. I couldn't have been eight years old. No one searches a station wagon with kids in it for weed. At least not back in the 1960s. It was a good cover and lucrative business for Uncle Aaron, until he ended up catching one in the back of the head in a home invasion robbery, though they didn't call it that back then.

"Bonnie never mentioned it." That was my cousin. His wife for three months.

"She would have been four."

"Stupid," Dale said. "I'm trying to find out if this is a job you can do and you're trying out comedy bits." Dale spit on his own floor. "So no one knows you there?"

"No one I'd recognize."

Dale opened up the envelope, shook out a set of car keys. "You have a driver's license?"

"Of course."

"Valid?"

"It'll pass," I said.

"In your name?"

"Come on, man," I said.

"I got an errand for you," he said. He handed me the car keys. "There's a Caddie in the parking lot. You drive it up to Seattle, drop off the keys, get a hotel for the night, catch the gray dog back to Klamath Falls. We'll give you five hundred plus whatever the hotel runs. Stay somewhere nice, even. Easy peasy."

"Whose Caddie is it?"

"No one you know," he said.

I got up and went to the window, see if I could spot the Caddie in question. The girls in the parking lot were sitting in their cars, doors open, bullshitting with each other—they all had pretty nice rides, Honda Accords, Toyota Camrys, a couple even had that new F-150 that looked so sleek in commercials—

waiting for any late-night customers, but not wanting to get rained on. Cops coming off their shifts. Doctors from the free clinic. They all liked to come by before we closed at two a.m.

"It's the red one," Dale said.

I recognized it. It belonged to a regular named Paul, who the girls in the lot called Poochie, because he owned Paws & Reflect, the dog-grooming place up over on Wantland Avenue. He tended to show up around dinner time covered in fine dog hair and smelling vaguely like pet shampoo. He'd get a burger, play some video poker, get a handjob, and head home. The girls said he did a nice job on their dogs, always gave them a good deal, even when there was a lot of mat work to be taken care of. I'd seen him maybe six times in the last month, but not recently.

One of the girls caught me watching her in the window. She went by Venus, but I would bet a C-note that her real name was something like Debbie. She had big Debbie vibes. I gave her a little wave. She flipped me a lazy bird.

"Nice ride," I said.

"Don't be thinking of running off with it," Dale said. He got up, looked out the window for a moment, then dropped the blinds. Dale went back to the sofa, put his feet up on the coffee table. "So you're good?"

"Who is 'we' in this situation?"

"What are you talking about?"

"You said, 'We'll give you five hundred.' Who is we?"

Dale shifted his weight on the sofa, which made a crackling sound. "You're just driving a car," he said. "You get to Seattle, you hand the keys to a little old lady, she hands you a cashier's check, you come home, we're all straight."

"A cashier's check?"

"She's a little old lady." He shrugged. "It was either that or like a dozen money orders."

"This doesn't sound straight."

Dale cleared his throat. "Between us?"

"No one else in the room."

"I've run into some trouble. Some money trouble. But I figured out a way through it. This is just the conclusion," Dale said. When I didn't respond, he continued, "Let me put it this way. You do this? Everything comes clean, we'll get you off the grill, get you into something more lucrative. Isn't that what you want? A shot? Isn't that why you called me when you needed a place to stay?"

At that moment, I had three hundred dollars hidden in my Dopp kit, a Nissan Sentra with West Virginia plates—a state I'd never visited—and a not-insignificant number of people looking for me in California who would be all too happy to get me into a wheelchair. They didn't want me dead. Dead men can't pay off their debts. A guy in a wheelchair, maybe he gets some state disability money. That's how these kinds of people think.

"When would I leave?" It was an eight-hour trip.

"You want some crank? You could leave right now."

"That shit makes me paranoid," I said.

"Oh, *that's* what makes you paranoid, okay." Dale looked at his watch. "Get a couple hours' sleep. Head out in the morning. Before sun-up, if you want to miss holiday traffic. That work for you?"

"What's the holiday?" I asked.

He pointed at a calendar from three years ago hanging on the wall. "It's Thanksgiving on Thursday, Mitch," he said. Today had started out as Tuesday but was now Wednesday morning.

"Well," I said, "in that case, I want a thousand. Up front. I'll find my own lodging."

Dale ran his tongue over his front teeth. It was a weird habit he had, from back when he had a habit. Then he shrugged. "Fuck it," he said and pulled out a wad of cash from the envelope, counted out ten bills. "Two things. Go the speed limit. You get pulled over, don't let anyone in the trunk."

☂

The eight-hour drive took me ten hours, the rain coming down in horizontal sheets until I pulled off Highway 5 in downtown Seattle, turned down East Madison, and in a few minutes found myself in a sun-dappled lakeside village filled with diagonal parking, artisan ice cream shoppes, too much green space, and women in Juicy track suits pushing strollers and sipping from Starbucks cups. It felt like I was in a Meg Ryan movie from the '90s, but not the one I'd actually seen. Everything was a shade of J. Crew. I fished the Post-it note Dale had given me with the directions to the address I was looking for and a few minutes and about a dozen strollers later, I found the Shore View at Madison Park, a six-story complex on 43rd that hung right over Lake Washington.

Dorothy Barker. Apartment 403.

I parked in the lot beside the building and then went back around front, buzzed Mrs. Barker's name on the keypad beside the lobby's door. Waited. Inside the double glass-front doors were two sofas, a coffee service with a platter of pastries on the table between them, copies of *People* and *Sunset* spread out artfully, like at a dental office. Back toward the bank of four elevators, a mailman was filling up a wall of mailboxes. Every thirty seconds or so, an old codger came out of the elevator, fished their mail out of their box and got back in before the elevator doors even had time to close.

Watching it was fucking hypnotic. Over five minutes, I saw ten, maybe fifteen tenants do the same exact move, like they were on a loop, until the mailman finished up, locked the boxes up and opened the front door, but didn't let me in.

"You trying to reach someone?" he said. He was about sixty, but still sinewy with muscle, and had that former military look, like a lot of mailmen, but had a spiderweb tattoo on his elbow that he tried to hide with an Ace joint sleeve. I showed him the Post-it. He nodded, like we agreed about something. "Ms. Barker didn't come down. Might be sleeping. You family?"

"Yeah," I said.

"Then why you got a Post-it?"

"Brain injury," I said. "No short-term memory."

The mailman gave me a once-over. I couldn't tell if he liked what he saw. "I let you in," he said, "you gotta promise not to rob the place." He pointed at a mirror above the buzzers. "There's a camera behind that. So, we got your face."

"Who is 'we'?"

"Government, eventually," the mailman said. "Building manager, though I doubt he gives a fuck."

"Well," I said, "that solves it. I won't rob the place."

The mailman shrugged. "She's a bit of a pill, anyway," he said, and held the door open for me.

☂

Apartment 403 was down a long hallway that smelled like cooking meat and cleaning solvent. There was a stack of three newspapers at the door, a Christmas wreath hung around the peephole, and even from outside I could hear the TV blaring. Someone was in the process of buying a vowel. I rang the doorbell. Waited. Knocked. Rang the doorbell again.

A door opened behind me. An old man in boxers, no shirt, and a Mariners cap stepped out, pushing a walker, holding a bag of trash, which also smelled like meat and cooking solvent. He looked at me for a few seconds, then said, "Get her to turn her damn TV down."

"I'd need her to come to the door," I said.

"She probably can't hear you over fucking Pat Sajak."

"You seen her?"

"No," he said. He scratched his chest. "You the son she's always talking about? Dog boy?"

"If I was, I'd have a key."

The old man shook his head. "Hold on." He dumped his

garbage bag on the floor, disappeared back into this apartment, and then returned a few minutes later holding a key looped to a spatula. "First ten years we lived here," he said, "we were on good terms. I'd water her plants when she went out of town, she'd feed my fish when I got happy feet."

"What happened?"

"My fish died," he said. He pushed his walker over to me, handed me the spatula. "And then my feet and knees and hips stopped cooperating."

"When was this?"

"Been another ten years," he said. "It's a good spatula, so I just kept it, but I guess she can have it back. I don't cook much these days."

I waited for the old man to disappear down the hall with his trash before I unlocked the door.

"Hello, Mrs. Barker?" I said. "I'm here with your car."

Nothing.

To the right was a short hallway leading to a bedroom, which is where the TV was playing. The door was open and I could see the corner of a bed and a dresser, but nothing else. In front of me was a great room, which was surrounded by floor-to-ceiling windows with a view of Lake Washington and the floating bridge to Bellevue.

I stepped a few feet in, sniffed. There was a bad smell some-where in the house. One I'd smelled a time or two before. I went down the hall, figured Mrs. Barker was in her bed or tub rotting away, but all I found in the bedroom was an immacu-lately made California King, covered with about fifty pillows, and an old-style TV, the kind that was also a piece of furniture, shoved into a corner. A woman in a floral dress was telling Pat Sajak about how she'd never been to Hawaii but that was all about to change!

I found the remote on the bedside table next to a glass of something brown. I clicked the TV off, smelled the glass. Coke or Pepsi. There was a dead fly in it and no carbonation. I took a look in the bathroom. The tub was empty. No one was dead on the toilet. So that was a relief. Opened the medicine cabinet. Found all the usual suspects. Klonopin. Xanax. Ambien. Percocet. Lipitor. Three different diuretics. Bystolic. Heparin. Nitroglycerin. I emptied the bottles of the good stuff into my pockets. A little something for the bus home. Found a hand towel, dampened it, wiped down everything I touched.

I made my way back down the hall, through a pocket door into a galley kitchen, found a Coke in the refrigerator, drank it down. Checked the milk. Good for another week. The yogurt. Same. There were green bananas on the counter. Back into the great room. The smell was stronger here. No blood on the floor. Maybe it was a dead rat in the wall? There was a sliding glass door to the patio, which wrapped around the apartment in an L. I opened it up, stepped outside, and found what I was looking for: There was a woman on a chaise lounge, a towel pulled up to her hips, hat and sunglasses on, a crow standing on her chest pecking at what was left of her fucking face.

☂

After wiping everything down, I found a cordless telephone in the kitchen, called Dale at home. When he didn't pick up there, I tried the office. "Everything good?" he asked.

"Mrs. Barker," I said. "You know her?"

"Not…directly." Whatever the fuck that meant.

"Okay, well, she's dead."

"What do you mean she's dead?"

"I mean there's a bird eating her fucking face. Dead."

"How long?"

I walked over to the sliding glass door, looked at Mrs. Barker. She hadn't started to liquefy but bugs were starting to work at the open bits, plus of course the birds. The weather had been fairly cool and the patio was somewhat protected from the elements by a wide over-hang, so that was a help. "A day or two."

I heard Dale light a cigarette. "That's a real problem."

"For who?"

"You see a cashier's check anywhere?"

"Not in plain sight."

"Open some drawers. See if maybe you can find a check-book."

"Let me ask you a question," I said, "you of the opinion you want my fingerprints all over this apartment? Because I'm not."

"You on her phone?"

"I am."

"Probably gonna be pretty clear she wasn't making calls today, so you've already fucked up, hoss. For both of us."

Shit.

"What do you want me to do?"

"Best thing would be to find that cashier's check. Second-best thing, figure out if she has a safe or some diamonds or something. Anything easy to move."

"You think I can just move a safe?"

"I think you can do whatever you want," Dale said, "but that maybe you've gone light on me."

"Light? I did five at San Quentin and don't want to go back. So don't talk to me about light."

"Look around," Dale said. "Find what you can find. I'm gonna need to call you back in fifteen minutes. Don't leave."

I found some cold cuts in the fridge, a loaf of Jewish rye, made myself a sandwich, flipped through a *People* magazine I found in the living room. It was from six months ago, so no one was worried about terrorists or flying or anything. Just celebrities doing celebrity shit. Poked around for a safe, or some stash of expensive jewels. Found some shoeboxes filled with receipts, a couple of old rings that someone would miss if they were gone, that kind of family heirloom shit that I was averse to stealing. Mrs. Barker's purse, which had some credit cards and thirty-six bucks in it and a sleeve of photos, all of a German shepherd. I took the credit cards, left the cash and the photos. Went through some drawers in the kitchen, found photos of Mrs. Barker with the same giant German shepherd. Found photos of Paul with the same giant German shepherd. Got up, went into her bedroom. Opened drawers. Nothing of value. Looked under the bed, half expecting to find the German shepherd rotting away, but there was nothing but dust bunnies and socks.

After twenty minutes, I called Dale back. Nobody picked up. Twenty-five minutes, I called the general line at the Purple Flamingo. The day assistant manager, a guy everyone called Prison Jack because all he ever talked about was his time in prison, like he was the only person who'd ever done time, picked up.

"I was hoping it was you," he said. "Can you come in this afternoon?"

"I'm just looking for Dale."

"Aren't you cellies with him?"

"Yeah," I said, "I was hoping to catch him."

"He didn't tell you? He quit."

"When?"

"Just now. Ten fucking minutes ago. Gabarians are gonna be pissed. He's really putting me in a..." I hung up before Prison Jack had time to finish his sentence.

☂

When I got to the parking lot, there was a teenage girl leaning against the Caddie, licking an ice cream cone. She was dressed in all black, thick white pancake make-up on her face, black lipstick, hair teased like she'd recently been electrocuted. She stared at me with vague interest when I walked up and hit the key fob to unlock the car.

"You're not Paul," she said. She was wearing a T-shirt that had the logo of a band, I presumed, called Christian Undead Necro Teens. She was maybe seventeen.

"Isn't it too cold to be eating ice cream?" I said. The sun had disappeared and the rain I'd driven in all day was beginning to sprinkle onto Madison Park.

"Oh god, no." The Christian Undead Necro Teen shrugged and rolled her eyes at the same time. It seemed to be the most physically taxing thing she'd ever done. "It's like how you're not supposed to go to bed with wet hair. None of that shit is real. There's no rules."

I looked up at the apartment building, see if I could make out Mrs. Barker's balcony, but the angle, thankfully, was wrong. Which was probably why no one had noticed her up there. "You live here?"

"No," Christian Undead Necro Teen said. "We're just here for Thanksgiving. My nana lives on the third floor, so I saw the car pull up. Thought it was Paul. But guess not."

"What's your shirt about?" I said.

"Christian Undead Necro Teens? That's my band. Not that we've recorded anything. But we will. Get on SubPop. Become bigger than Nirvana ever was, but like, live to spend the money."

"Good plan," I said. "How do you know Paul?"

"We hang out sometimes during the summer," she said. "He's real cool." This made her laugh. "Well, okay, not *cool*, but like, nice. Not a creeper." Then she laughed again. It was like she was having a conversation with someone else and I just happened to be standing there, too. "Well, okay, like, probably a creeper, but not like a pedo creeper. When he's here at the holidays and we're here, he'll always drive me to Pioneer Square and like pick me up and take me for Cow Chip Cookies and all that."

"What's 'all that' entail?"

Chritian Undead Necro Teen eyed me for a moment, then said, "You a cop?"

"I look like a cop?"

"Undercover, maybe." She licked her cone. "He helps me sell my Adderall and Xanax and shit. Normal kid stuff. My loser mom is trying to turn me into an addict. So I'm turning a profit on it."

"That's no way to talk about your mom."

"She's not much of a mother." She pointed at the Caddie. "Like, that's really Paul's mom's car, I guess? But she's too old to enjoy it, that's what he told me, so like, it's fun for him to drive me around." She shrugged again, this time as if there was a thousand-pound yoke over her shoulders. "My mom went to high school with Paul, so it's like, whatever. He's like an uncle."

"Where's your mom now?"

"She and my nana are screaming at each other upstairs. So I decided to get a cone and wait it out, hoping Paul would see me and come save the day. But guess not." She took another lick of her cone and then tossed it into a bush. In the distance, I thought I heard a siren. Probably just a coincidence. The Christian Undead Necro Teen took a cell phone from her purse, but didn't do anything with it. "She'll think I've been abducted again if she notices I'm gone, so I guess I better call her at some point."

"Again?"

"Last summer got crazy."

The siren got louder. I took a step out onto the street, looked down the block, then back toward Madison Street. On the corner, a woman stood talking on her cell phone, pushing a stroller back and forth with her foot. Except there was a corgi in the stroller, not a kid. The corgi heard the siren, too, his head up, ears perked. I needed to get the fuck out of Madison Park.

"Why are you driving Paul's car?" Christian Undead Necro Teen asked.

"I was just dropping it off," I said.

"That doesn't make sense," she said, but with no real conviction behind it, even though she was correct. It didn't make any

110

sense. "How old are you?" she asked.

"Old enough not to be comfortable with this conversation," I said. "How old are you?"

"I'll be nineteen," she said. She didn't give a timeline. "I don't suppose you want to drive me to Pioneer Square, do you?"

"Sorry, kid," I said. "I'm not the kind of guy you're supposed to ask for rides."

A police cruiser turned down 43rd The sirens blared for a moment and then abruptly turned off, leaving just the spinning lights. The cruiser came to a stop in front of the Shore View but the cop stayed in his seat.

"Ugh, my mom probably already called 911," she said. Christian Undead Necro Teen flashed me a peace sign. "See you never."

She was about ten yards away when I shouted, "What's your name?"

"Sylvia," she said, not turning around.

"That's an old-lady name," I said.

"Maybe I'm really an old lady," she said and then she, too, flipped me off.

"Friend of yours?"

I turned and the cop was out of his cruiser now, watching me, a bemused look on his face.

"Just met," I said. We both watched her stroll another twenty yards or so up the block, then plop down on a bench with a view of Lake Washington.

"Never got that goth shit," the cop said. "Like why pretend to be dead? So weird."

A window opened on the third floor of the building. A woman stuck her head out, shouted, "Finally! They're making me crazy!" and then closed the window.

"You live here?" the cop asked.

"Nope," I said. "Just dropped something off."

The cop adjusted his belt. "Lived in Seattle my whole life," he said, "seen this building a thousand times, never been inside. Isn't that weird." Not a question. Just a statement.

"It's like that sometimes," I said.

"Nice ride," he said and then he disappeared inside the building.

I popped open the trunk once he was gone. It was empty, save for a white Igloo cooler. I took the top off. There were several ice packs stacked on top of something. I peeled away the top layer and that's when I saw the pointed ears, the long snout, the dead eyes.

The German shepherd.

So that's where he was. There was a Post-it note stuck to his head. It read, in all-caps: NEXT TIME IT WILL BE YOUR SUN IF YOU DON'T PAY UP.

Fucking Dale couldn't spell for shit.

I repacked everything, closed the trunk, locked the Caddie, walked up the block, found Sylvia, sat down next to her. She was smoking a clove cigarette, offered me a drag.

"I was told they make your lungs bleed," I said.

"I heard that, too," she said. "That like they have fiberglass in them or something. But that's not true."

"No?"

"Think about it," she said. "Could they really sell them if they did?"

She had a point. "Give me one," I said. Lit it up. Inhaled. It was like smoking a yoga mat dipped in formaldehyde. I dug the keys out of my pocket. "You want to get out of here?" I asked.

"Like nothing else in the world," she said.

"You do me a favor?" I asked.

Sylvia took a long drag on her clove. "I'm actually fifteen."

"You know how to drive?"

She took another drag. "And a half. Fifteen and a half."

"Yes or no," I said.

"I'm in driver's ed," she said.

I handed her the keys and a couple of Mrs. Barker's credit

cards, all of which she took without question. "How much you think you could get for those cards?"

"They're not reported stolen?"

"No."

She took a drag from the clove. "Kids at the Square will go nuts on these. But not if you're around." She flipped over a gold American Express card. "You could buy a plane with this, probably."

"I need about three grand," I said. Three grand, I could get a plane ticket home, have some walking-around money for a few days, give my mom some cash back, start making good on things. Sleep in my old bedroom. Maybe hawk my old Star Wars toys for extra cash while I waited on the next thing.

"When?"

"How soon you think you could get it for me?"

"Two, three hours," she said. "Oooh, this is nice." She waved a Nordstrom card in the air.

"It's all yours. Finder's fee."

"How long?"

"Couple days, I'd guess." Another cop car came down the street, lights rolling, but no sirens, parked in front of the Shore View.

"My mom for sure called the cops," Sylvia said.

"How about we drive downtown," I said, "you drop me off, come back with the money, and we're square."

"How do you know I'll show back up?"

"Well," I said, "I know where your nana lives. I presume you don't want her to wash up somewhere."

Sylvia smiled. She had perfect teeth. I'd bet she lived in a house worth about a million dollars somewhere. "You're so much more interesting than Paul," she said.

Sylvia dropped me off near Pike Place Market, because I like the mood of tourist traps and the smell of raw fish, told me she'd be back in ninety minutes. I found a clam chowder spot down the block, got a bread bowl, watched the rain fall into Lake Washington, tried Dale's cell phone. Rodney Gabarian answered it.

"Motherfucker," Rodney said.

"Easy with that motherfucker business," I said. I was still feeling bad about running out on my mom. "I'm presuming Dale isn't with you?"

"Motherfucker," he said, "it's just a figure of speak. I own this phone. Corporate perk. Asshole left it behind. Where are you?"

"I'm having some clam chowder," I said. "Taking a vacation day in Seattle."

"Lucky you," he said. "My brother is in Seattle too. Maybe he can come by and chat with you. Why don't you give me the address."

"Sure," I said and gave him the address of the Shore View.

"Your motherfucker friend departed Klamath Falls," he said, "with my money. Cleaned out the safe and all the registers."

"Not my problem."

"Motherfucker, I know you were literally helping him with some dumb shit. This dumb scam he had working. Which was to pay back a previous loan he had to me, so understand this is a double loss on my part." He paused. In the background, some Christmas music began playing. Johnny Mathis. A classic. "Nice hi-fi here in Dale's den. What do you think I could get for it?"

"That's mine," I said. "Maybe twenty-five bucks."

"Nothing is worth shit anymore." Off went Johnny Mathis. "You sleep on this Murphy bed in the den?"

"I do."

"Then I will not piss on it."

"I feel like I'll be moving."

"I respect you," Rodney said, "but you're not making any

plans for a while, motherfucker. This house. There any secret hiding places?"

I had to think for a minute. "There's an entrance to the crawl space in the hall closet," I said. "Only thing down there are raccoons and kit fox pups."

"Kit fox pups?"

"I heard them crying the other day," I said.

"You *are* a dumb motherfucker." Rodney laughed for a few seconds. "Did you see these foxes?"

I hadn't. I'd just woken up one night last week and heard them mewing and went back to sleep. The next morning Dale told me what was what.

"I'll call Animal Control if you like," Rodney said. "I have a feeling this will be an experience you'll want to be here for." I heard a car door open and close. An engine start up. "Your cousin stole about fifty Gs from the Purple Flamingo."

"Cousin-in-law," I said. "Ex."

"Family is family," he said. "I presume you have some money that now belongs to me?"

"That didn't work out."

"No?"

"Lady was dead when I got there."

"How?"

"I'd guess eighty years of fatty foods," I said.

Rodney laughed. "Ah, that explains that. My advice, motherfucker? Make good choices. Come back to Klamath Falls. I'll let you work off the debt. I'm not unreasonable. Run, you'll always be running. You don't want that."

☂

Forty-five minutes later, which was a full thirty minutes late, Sylvia walked into the clam chowder spot holding two huge Nordstrom's bags, sat down across from me, picked up my spoon, dug some damp bread out of my bowl, swallowed it down. "That's good."

"Always get the bread bowl," I said. "That's my motto."

"So," she said. She dug another hunk of bread out. "The car got stolen." She reached into her jacket pocket, came out with a handful of cash, set it on the table between us. I counted it. There was about five grand there.

"A terrible shame," I said.

"I told the thieves they had forty-eight hours."

"You're going to be a real problem for your parents," I said.

"My mom finally called me," she said. She reached into her bag, pulled out a man's shirt, a heavy coat, sport coat, slacks, some socks, a beanie, even a new watch. A Movado. Nice. "Crazy, neighbors found Mrs. Barker dead on her patio."

"You don't say."

"Someone called the building manager, I guess."

"That sounds like a person who made a good choice."

"Well," Sylvia said, "anywho, I thought you might want a new outfit. In case you needed to not meet any descriptions of you."

"I didn't kill her," I said. "That's not the kind of person I am anymore."

"Anymore?"

"It was nice meeting you, Sylvia." I extended my hand. She shook it, firmly, while staring directly into my eyes. Good manners went a long way with me, especially with kids.

"When I tell my friends this," Sylvia said, "it won't be so clear cut." She stood up. "Weird day, yeah?"

"It's been a dog's year."

She started out the restaurant, then stopped, like she realized she'd forgotten something, came back to the table. "You reminded me," she said. "Whoever killed that dog, that's fucked up. It's irredeemable to kill a dog. You can't even do that in a book or in a movie. You know? You shouldn't abide that. Whatever you are."

"I don't," I said.

"And I guess, Paul, too?"

"Yeah," I said. "He's dead. I'm sorry about that."

"Why are you so casual?"

"I've done a lot of bad shit in my life. Today is not the worst of it. I didn't know Paul like you did. He's just a guy who made friends with the wrong people. That should be a lesson for you."

Sylvia took that in, then shrugged. "Anywho. What are you going to do about it?"

"I've been sitting here trying to figure that out."

"I vote revenge." She gave me the peace sign again. "See you never."

That night, I took the last Greyhound out of Seattle, which was a red-eye to Walla Walla, where I still had some family, if you count dead people as family. My grandparents were buried there along with a handful of cousins. I hadn't been back in decades, but when I saw it on the destination board, it was the one place that made any sense to me. I swallowed a handful of Mrs. Barker's pills and fell into a hallucinogenic sleep in which I dreamt that I dug up my grandmother and stole diamond rings off her skeleton and then I had to fight Marcus Whitman to the death.

When I woke up, we were just outside the Wallula Junction, the Snake River black in the darkness. I dug out my cell phone and made a few calls: I left a message on my mother's voicemail, letting her know I was still alive, so she didn't have a shitty Thanksgiving. I called the Klamath Falls Natural Gas Services emergency hotline and reported a leak at Dale's address. If Paul was in the crawl space, they'd find him. And then I called the Purple Flamingo and left a message on the voicemail, letting them know I was quitting and where to send my check. I gave them my sister's address.

That would keep everyone busy for a while.

I went into the bus's shitter and snapped my phone into pieces, dumped everything into the toilet. It was 5:12 a.m. I had about four grand left, after buying some luggage and the bus ticket. Not enough to start a new life, but enough to get from one bad situation to the next. I also had a few of Mrs. Barker's credit cards, which might be good for another couple days. But that was it.

I stepped out of the bathroom and examined the bus. I counted fifty-three people, all asleep. We were forty minutes from Walla Walla. If I moved quickly and quietly, I could probably get a dozen wallets, not that Greyhound passengers were known for their amazing wealth. But that wasn't the point. I'd need a new ID for a while and with enough time and enough driver's licenses, I could make some passable magic. Not magic enough to get on a plane, but enough to cash some bad checks, get some walking-around money, a rental car, maybe get down to Reno, double my money, meet a nice girl, get married, start fresh.

Or just find someone who could get me a gun.

☂☂☂

OIL AND WATER
Smita Harish Jain

R oger McElroy dropped the thermometer, sending jiggly
blobs of mercury skittering across his workspace. He still
used the old-fashioned kind in his lab because they were the
best way to validate the autoclaves he used to sterilize the
equipment that he and his team needed to complete their
research. The lab, located in the eastern Strait of Juan de Fuca,
near the city of Port Townsend, was funded by wealthy conser-
vationists who wanted to do more with their money than buy
beach property and yachts. Their mission was to protect the
aquatic ecosystems of the Strait and the marine life that made
the area its home. As the senior scientist at the Save the Orcas
Foundation, he should have known to be more careful.

"Shit!"

Roger grabbed a pair of rubber gloves and a sheet of paper
and pushed the beads of mercury into one big ball. With the
edge of the paper, he slid the ball into a glass test tube, then
capped it and placed it in a rack on a high shelf. He wiped the
surface of the table with sulfur powder, his hands still shaking
from what he had just avoided. A few minutes is all it would
have taken for the exposed mercury to evaporate into the air
and become toxic enough to kill him.

He opened all the windows in the small space to clear any
lingering vapor, and that's when he heard it. The same low,

desperate squeal he had heard three other times in the past few years. He snatched up his medical kit and ran from the lab to the water's edge, praying that this time would turn out differently.

A thick circle of gawkers had formed on the grass and rocks just beyond the narrow shoreline. "Move! Please, move," he shouted and pushed his way through them until he burst into the center.

Alana, his lead research assistant, was the first to speak.

"I was out hiking the trails, and I found her here. It's L42," she said, pointing at the Africa-shaped saddle patch behind the prostrate orca's dorsal fin.

Being able to identify the members of the three pods of southern resident orcas that inhabited the waters of Puget Sound by only their markings was a skill, if not a requirement, shared by all of Roger's lab workers. He himself had been recording every movement, birth, illness, death, and matriline of the pods that he could, for almost thirty years.

Roger looked past the markings—he had already identified the orca from her wails—and traced a straight line from her dorsal fin to her engorged midsection. He and his team had been safeguarding the precious cargo for the better part of eighteen months, tracking the whale and monitoring her vitals through fecal samples they skimmed off the water's surface. If they could help her carry to term, the calf would be the first one born to L-pod in more than five years.

He ran his fingers over her protruding belly, trying to calm her with his practiced touch, while his team used a fire hose and buckets of water from the Strait of Juan de Fuca to keep her from drying out on the hot stones.

"There's also this," Alana said, and pointed to three parallel scratches near L42's fin.

The scientists who studied the southern residents used alpha-numeric names to identify them—the letters, J, K, or L indicating their pod affiliation, and the numbers giving the order of their birth.

"Raking scars," Roger confirmed.

"Do you think she got into a tussle with another orca and tried to escape and ended up stranded here?" Alana asked, wiping away tears. She had been with him for almost ten years and had seen the loss of the last three orcas. She had vowed that she would do anything to keep from losing another one.

Roger shook his head. "Those scratches wouldn't weaken her to this level. There's got to be something else going on."

When L42 settled into a regular breathing pattern, Roger called for the stretcher and, while he waited, drew blood from the animal to confirm what he already feared. He sent Alana back to the lab to start the analysis and, with the help of his team and a few of the onlookers, rolled L42 onto the canvas and eased her back into the Strait, waiting with her until she had enough support from the water itself to refloat and make her way back to her pod. After a few minutes of lying in the water to gather her strength, she rolled onto her side, flapped her tail a few times, and swam away to the cheers of the onlookers.

Roger released the breath he had been holding and collapsed onto the rock formations near the shore. The skies had darkened early, and the atlas cedars and mountain ashes that lined the perimeter of the beach swayed violently in the winds of an impending storm. The waves throbbed against the shore, warning even the most ardent beachgoers to stay back. Something bad had happened there, and Roger would make sure it never happened again.

When Alana heard him enter the lab, she looked up from the hematology microscope in front of her and turned to face him. "It's mercury," she said, her shoulders dropping in resignation.

🌂

"Two years ago, a tanker carrying one-and-a-half million gallons of crude oil ran aground trying to navigate the Rosario

Strait in dense fog and tore several long holes in its hull. By the time a response team got to it and finished transferring the oil to another tanker, a quarter of a million gallons had already seeped into the water. The spill stretched into the Strait of Juan de Fuca and not only contaminated the orca pods that forage there, but also reached their primary food source, the Chinook salmon that feed there before returning to their home waters to spawn. All that dilbit contained mercury, and that mercury is still part of their habitat."

"What's dilbit?" Craig, the lab's newest research tech, asked when Roger was done explaining what had caused L42 to become disoriented and end up on the rocks outside the water.

Alana took over. "Dilbit, diluted bitumen, is a kind of crude oil that contains high levels of mineral pitch—think asphalt. If it spills, it doesn't just contaminate the surface of the water, it sinks to the bottom and attaches to the sediment on the sea floor, which makes it practically impossible to clean up. The orcas and the salmon live with that poison and, if enough of it builds up, it eventually kills them."

"If InterCoastal Oil's proposed pipeline expansion goes through, hundreds more tankers will cross from British Columbia down the Pacific Coast," Roger said.

"Which will make the chances of more spills of dilbit and other crude oils go way up," Craig surmised.

"And the population of the orcas go way down," Sarah, the other tech, finished.

All four members of the research team sat in silence, contemplating the full import of L42's beaching and what it represented for the eighty or so southern residents that still remained.

Finally, Alana said, "We can't afford to lose any more orcas, let alone a pregnant one."

"Alana's right. What are we going to do, Dr. McElroy?" Sarah asked.

Roger shook his head, wondering the same thing.

"I know!" Craig exclaimed. "The orcas are endangered. Even the Chinook are on the endangered list. That should be enough to keep the expansion from going through." He grinned, as if he had just solved cold fusion.

Alana and Roger exchanged a knowing look.

"I've tried that already, a few times, ever since the southern residents went on that list in 2005," Roger said.

"Besides, the company the State Department hired to do the feasibility study cooked their results. As far as anyone can tell from their findings, there'll be no impact to the southern resident population as a result of the expansion," Alana added.

"Why don't we just tell them the research is wrong?" Sarah asked.

"We don't have any proof, other than three dead orcas. That's not going to be enough to take on Big Oil and their PACs," Alana said.

"The government has spent tens of millions of dollars on this study and has zero incentive to question it or have it re-done, based simply on our word," Roger said.

The mood in the lab went from hopeful to despondent.

"We have to do something," Sarah said. "I waitress at the country club a few days a week, and I see the executives from the oil companies in there all the time. Maybe you could come there and talk to them, Dr. McElroy."

☂

The dining room of the Vintage Hills Country Club in Seattle boasted Danish teak walls and Schonbek crystal chandeliers and a menu of the freshest salmon brought in daily from the eastern Strait of Juan de Fuca. When the CEOs of InterCoastal Oil and the research firm the State Department had hired, Deep Sea Labs, agreed to meet with Roger and his team, they suggested the club.

"This is quite a place," Roger said, impressed despite his best efforts not to be.

"Yes, and we can dine on the same food as your precious orcas do," said InterCoastal's head, Steve Springer, giving Roger yet another reason to hate him.

When Sarah brought over the menus, Springer waved them away, just as she had told Roger he would, when the team was discussing her idea.

"We don't need those. Bring us the baked king salmon with a side of coconut rice, and the lemon kale salad to start." Springer ordered for the table without checking with any of the others.

Roger signaled his team with a quick glance to let it go. They had bigger fish to fry.

"Make sure it's cooked with the skin side down," Springer demanded. "No one likes an overcooked salmon, am I right?" He winked at Sarah.

Putz, Roger thought but didn't say.

"Will that be all?" Sarah asked.

Springer looked her over, his tongue running along his upper lip. "For now," he said, patting her behind when she turned to walk to the kitchen.

Craig pushed his chair back and started to rise when Alana pulled him back. "Eye on the prize," she whispered. "We all have our parts to play."

Craig returned to his seat before the two men noticed.

"What do we need to say to convince you that the expansion is a good idea for everyone involved?" Springer said, looking at Craig, Alana, and Roger in turns.

The question confirmed Roger's worst fear. The two men hadn't come there to discuss the issue; they had come to placate his team. If they didn't, Roger's benefactors might use their deep pockets to turn the expansion into a public relations nightmare for their companies or, worse, tie up the project in the courts, at least temporarily. Still, the two men were there, and this was the team's chance—its only chance—to reason with them. Roger would start with the smaller of his two complaints and hope it would be enough to sway them.

"The Save the Orcas Foundation is concerned about the increased tanker traffic your proposed expansion will bring to the area," Roger started.

"Specifically, we are concerned about the noise level," Alana added.

"Noise level? Shouldn't you be having this conversation with the whale-watching boats?" Greg Anderson, the CEO of Deep Sea, launched right into what seemed to Roger to be a familiar re-direct, one Anderson had probably used many times before, to avoid answering the question.

"The boats are not the issue. Their noise level is nothing compared to—" Roger started to say but was cut off by Springer.

"Sure, they are. You've got thousands of whale tours a year in Puget Sound and, what, forty-five or fifty oil tankers?"

Was this guy being intentionally stupid, or did he think Roger was stupid?

"There's a big difference between a hundred-person catamaran and a thousand-foot oil tanker capable of carrying a hundred-and-twenty-five thousand deadweight tons." Roger couldn't keep the anger out of his voice. Alana kicked him under the table.

"The sound of the tanker engines can cover up the whales' communications and make it harder for them to hear each other." She tried to bring down the temperature with an explanation.

"That's how they distinguish their prey from other orcas," Craig said.

"With the increased noise from the tankers, the orcas will stop hunting and even mating. If this population has any prayer of survival, it needs to mate," Alana said.

"Don't we all?" Springer said and slapped his knee.

Alana ignored his comment. "As it is, a female can give birth only once every three to five years, sometimes only once every ten years. The noise from the additional tankers will slow down this rate even more."

"Can they even hear the noise five hundred feet below the water's surface?" Anderson asked, sounding bored.

"Yes, they can. Besides, they have to surface at least every fifteen minutes to get air, so they're not always that low," Roger said.

He and his team exchanged a quick glance. They were definitely not dealing with the brain trust here. These men understood nothing about what their companies did, except the bottom line.

"Besides, the whale watchers aren't poisoning the orcas with what they're dropping into the Strait," Alana said, now just as angry as Roger.

"If you go through with this expansion, that forty-five or fifty number is going to grow to well over three hundred," Craig said. "Three hundred tankers a year are going to cross the Strait and the Salish Sea beyond it, and who knows how many more accidents that'll mean."

Neither man responded. Instead, they turned to their own conversation. Roger was left with no other choice than to bring up the rumors.

"Your report"—he turned to Anderson when he said this— "failed to take into account the impact of the increased traffic on the southern resident population. Without a complete environmental impact assessment, your report might not get approved." He knew that wasn't true, but he was going to see how far he could take it. Maybe if he got them to admit to falsifying their research, he wouldn't have to go through with the rest of the plan.

Unfortunately, Anderson had a ready answer. "Not having it in there just means there wouldn't be any additional impact. It isn't like InterCoastal's tankers are the only ones in the water. If it's not theirs, it'll be someone else's. All the vessel traffic in Puget Sound is not going to stop if the expansion goes away."

These men were being purposely obtuse. Roger puffed his cheeks and blew out a long breath. He didn't know how much more of this he could take.

"We've got support from the locals who know that the expansion will add another two thousand jobs to the economy. We're also putting aside fifteen million dollars to help repopulate the salmon hatcheries. We're even setting up three new response bases along the routes taken by our tankers. What more do you expect us to do? It's already overkill, and all just to satisfy the tree-huggers."

Springer's use of a generic term to describe all environmentalists grated Roger's nerves, but that was the least of the man's offenses.

"By the time your response teams get to a spill—which could be hundreds of miles away from the base—the dilbit will already have settled into the sediment at the bottom of the sea. No response team is going to matter at that point." Alana found herself shouting at the two CEOs.

"What you're not getting is that once these few remaining pods die, there will never be any more southern resident orcas in the world, ever." Craig tried to appeal to their compassion for posterity.

Just then, Sarah returned with a cart and seven plates of the king salmon, five on the top shelf and two on the bottom. She looked at Roger just long enough to see him nod—so slightly as to barely register—and placed the plates from the lower shelf before the two CEOs. She served the others from the remaining five plates and, when everybody had their meals, Craig continued.

"This is the only place the southern residents can find food. They need the Chinook to survive."

"Just like us!" Springer said and shoved a huge piece of the fish from his plate down his gullet, barely chewing it before he swallowed.

"You're worrying about a leak that hasn't even happened," Anderson said, tucking into his own meal. "Even if it does, how big is the leak compared to how big the ocean is?" Anderson pinched the thumb and forefinger of his left hand together to indicate the size of a potential spill, then stretched out both arms as wide as he could to indicate the water traversed by the tankers.

"Greg is right. You're making way too much out of this," Springer said. "Besides, it's not like a single human has ever gotten hurt because of an oil spill," he said around a mouthful of the salmon.

☂

A week later, the bodies of Steve Springer and Greg Anderson turned up in the parking lot of the Vintage Hills Country Club, right next to their cars. The autopsies showed their last meal had been baked king salmon with a side of coconut rice. "They ordered it three or four times a week," the restaurant's manager told the police. "In fact, they ordered it just today. We all knew it was their favorite." And that the salmon had dangerous levels of mercury in it.

"The Deep Sea Labs' report showed no evidence of any mercury deposits still remaining from the last crude oil spill in the Juan de Fuca Strait," the State Department spokesman told the reporters who had gathered at the site. "But these deaths tell a different story. We will be doing a full investigation to determine if it is actually safe for the pipeline expansion to go through. Now, it's about more than sea life. Human lives could also be in danger."

As Roger and his team drove back to the lab, Sarah said, "The funny thing about mercury is, even though it can kill you, you don't always know it's coming. It doesn't have a smell or a taste."

"That's true," Craig said. "So, it can build up to a dangerous level, before you even realize it."

"Just like happened to the last three orcas who died," Alana said.

Roger said nothing. He didn't need to.

☂

At the end of the summer, the team returned to the rocky shore where they had found L42 almost three months before. The water was a royal blue that day, a far cry from the angry gray of the last time they had been there. All around them, ducks and gulls made themselves known, and bikers cruised down the pathways. The sun had burned off the morning fog, and from where the team had spread its blankets on a small grassy patch near the shoreline, they had clear views of both the Olympic Mountains and Mount Rainier. But they had come to see something else.

"Look! There they are!" Sarah was on her feet, jumping up and down.

They all followed her finger and caught L42 just as she was jumping out of the water, a small orca jumping right behind her.

"Welcome, L125!" they said in unison.

☂☂☂

SMASH & GRAB
Charles Philipp Martin

They ease the F-150 into the lot, Eudy driving because Eudy has the license. Gullick rides shotgun as they back up the tailgate to face the window of T&J Quikstop.

"Get out," Eudy says as he pulls on his ski mask.

"What?" Gullick's mask is already on, hiding his telltale ginger hair.

"Get out. Take the chain."

Not a good sign that Gullick's already forgotten this part of the plan. Get out before I crash in. That way you won't get pinned inside if the truck door gets stuck. You'll be able to move.

Gullick jumps out and stands back as Eudy throws it into reverse and punches the throttle. Two, maybe two and a half tons of Ford slam into the window, taking out the glass. Gullick hops through the store window, fifty pounds of chain in the drum clutched to his chest, barely slowing him down. The kid is strong and fast, which is why Eudy chose him.

Eudy throws open his own door, bashing a pastry rack, sending it flying into a cooler. By the time he reaches the back wall Gullick has the drum open and is pulling out yards of chain hand-over-hand. In two minutes they've wrapped the chain in loops around the ATM. Another two minutes and they'll be hoisting it into the truck bed so they can haul ass out of there, richer by ten grand or so. Eudy knows the machine is

131

crammed with money. This afternoon he tailed the van from the cash management company that refills these things, watched it hit the Quikstop at five.

Gullick glances out the remains of the store window.

"Nothing yet."

"White Center, broken glass at two a.m.? No one gives a shit." White Center is an unincorporated little district just south of Seattle but still served by the city, sort of. It draws Vietnamese, Somalis, Filipinos, all kinds of people who share a desire to Keep to Themselves.

"Don't hear the alarm."

"Sometimes you're lucky," Eudy says while shackling the chain to the frame. "They didn't set it, or it doesn't go off, whatever. But you can't be sure. So let's get it done!"

They double-time through a swamp of candy and snacks, leap into the idling truck, and Eudy guns the engine. Tires spin, then smoke, but the pickup doesn't move. He guns it again. Nothing but noise and the stink of burning rubber.

Turns out the ATM's base is a steel plate anchored to the floor with six bolts, three-quarter-inch by the look of them. The truck can't budge it. Must be a new model—the maker saw someone like Eudy coming.

"Shit," hisses Gullick, kicking the unit in anger. "Shoulda looked before. That ain't goin' nowhere."

"Get in."

Once again Gullick obeys, and Eudy steps on the gas, this time with the truck in reverse. The rear of the truck smashes into the ATM, the impact launching both men into the dash. For a moment they're stunned, and then they check out the machine behind them.

It's on a tilt now; one more good whack should do it. This time they fasten their seat belts and Eudy rolls the truck forward to the window edge, then reverses it again into the cash machine, hard.

Too hard. The truck barrels into the machine, knocks it over and keeps going until its rear wheels lift a foot off the floor. Now the vehicle is tilted up, the rear end off the ground, perched atop the ATM as if on jack stands. The two men stare dumbly out the windshield at nothing but linoleum floor.

"Shit!"

Eudy bats the shift lever into D and gives it gas. The rear wheels whine uselessly. He slaps it into R. Same.

"Shit! Shit! SHIT!" he shouts, thumping the steering wheel so hard it hurts. Why hadn't he checked for all-wheel drive when he boosted the ride from the Woodland Park Zoo lot this afternoon?

"What now, man?" says Gullick. For not the first time Eudy wonders if he was wise to take a fifteen-year-old along. The kid wants the cash to get, among other things, braces.

They scan the lot outside. Still empty. The Seattle cop shortage is a good thing.

"We go."

"Without the cash?"

"Now!"

If they can make it out of there, they should be home free. Eudy insisted on gloves and ski masks; no prints, nothing worthwhile on surveillance video. They'll both chuck any identifiable clothing. He's done a few of these, and learned from mistakes, his own and those of others too.

They freeze at the sound of a voice from the dark outside.

"Stay there!" shouts someone. A male voice.

"Who's that?" says Gullick.

"Who cares?" says Eudy. "Go!"

They dash for the store window but a man appears and blocks the way. Not too tall, wide-shouldered, with light brown skin and a frigid stare. His fingers snake and writhe around an aluminum baseball bat as if he's itching, itching to take a swing.

"Don't try it! The police are coming! Move and I'll break you!"

A slight accent. Latino, maybe? Eudy doesn't know or care.

He sizes up the man. Maybe thirty, conservative haircut, an intelligent face in his big round head. Good biceps, triceps, and more important, eyes that, like his own, are sweeping the room, taking in everything, feeding it into the brain so that he's ready for the next move.

"There's two of us, man," says Gullick.

The guy shakes his head. "One of me and this is enough," he says, jiggling the bat. "Don't try it." He steps into the store, kicks aside a box of protein bars, and faces them. He's no security guard, not a cop, not with those cuffed gray pants and tucked-in long-sleeve blue shirt. Maybe a car salesman or something.

But those biceps.

Eudy gets his first idea: the farther apart he and Gullick are, the less likely this guy can handle them both. He backs to one side.

"I said *stay there*!" But Eudy keeps backing up. The guy shifts his eyes from one man to the other, obviously trying to keep both of them on his radar.

Gullick is the first to jump. But not at the guy. He lunges away from them both and dives toward the window. The man starts for Gullick, bat raised, but then Eudy heads straight for him, gets his attention. The guy turns back to block Eudy, the bird in hand. Eudy backs up a couple of steps. Gullick melts into the dark.

For a minute they stare at each other. Then the guy speaks.

"Take off your mask."

Eudy does nothing.

"It's over. Take off the mask."

Eudy is looking everywhere, over the man's shoulder for cops, around the store for a possible weapon. Nothing.

"What's this to you?" Eudy asks. "This your store?"

"Nope."

"You work here?"

The man shakes his head no. "But I work. Not like you. Not

like your loser friend who ran off, leavin' your ass hangin'."

"Did plenty of working. Doesn't pay, you know?"

"Maybe you don't know how to work. You know why I'm here this late?"

Eudy says nothing.

"I was working. Two a.m. and I'm working."

Eudy comes up with a faint smile. "That's how to get ahead, they tell me."

"Wiseass. But you know, you're right. You work hard, the country'll treat you good. The only problem is *you*. People like you who take and don't give anything back." His fingers twitch around the bat's handle.

Eudy steps forward. "Don't judge me, man, I..."

"Stay back! Oh, I don't judge you. The judge is goin' to do that. They'll put trash like you away, like you deserve."

Maybe he's trying to heat me up, Eudy thinks. Make me mad enough to jump him so he can play hero with the Louisville slugger. Ain't gonna happen. Think, think...

"Look," Eudy says finally. "You don't want to do this. I'm just tryin' to get some money together. I got a brother in college. He's learning HVAC."

The man lets out a derisive sniff. "So you gotta steal to send him to school?"

Still looking for something to match up with the baseball bat. A pipe, a hammer, something. But the place is a mess. If there's something around, it's hidden under the toppled racks of Fritos bags and Chips Ahoy boxes that the truck scattered when it busted through the window.

"No. We gotta pay the rent. Eighteen hundred a month."

"You're young. What are you, twenty-two?"

"Twenty-four."

"No one else working in your family? They all out robbing stores?"

"Yeah, no. My mom works at the pet store at a mall. Nineteen bucks an hour." Instantly Eudy regrets talking. *Will the*

135

cops try to find me through Mom? No, there are too many PetCos and PetSmarts.

"Can't you live on that? Need to steal from people?"

"After they take shit out, it's like, what? Twenty-six hundred a month. Pay rent, not much left, man."

"So who says you can't do better? I swear, you people drive me nuts. You won't make anything of yourselves."

"Yeah? What do you do?"

"I've got my own business. Don't depend on anyone, don't steal. Work my ass off."

"I'll bet you do, man."

Another sniff of contempt. "I've got my own real estate office. Up there." He thrusts a finger toward the ceiling. "Ortega Realty. That's me. You should check for upstairs tenants the next time you rob a place." He laughs. "Won't be for a while. Five or ten years..."

"I didn't do nothin' to you," Eudy says. "Let me go, man." He uses his best man-to-man tone. *Just us guys talkin', makin a deal. C'mon, you got this.*

"Nah, you did plenty. People like you ruin it for everyone. Property crime is killing Seattle."

"Yeah? You're doin' okay. You just said so."

"You know what your shit does to property values? No one wants to live where there's property crime, violence."

"Then why can't we buy a house? Can't even pay rent no more."

"Yeah, everyone's got a sad story."

"Hey, my mom used to work in Seattle. I grew up in Central. Then the tech bros started buying houses, prices go up, rents go up, and we gotta move down south to find something. My mom commuted to a hospital here from Federal Way till it got too much for her. She was a housekeeper, got benefits. Now she's sellin' cat litter for nineteen bucks an hour, no health insurance. That's on you."

"On me?"

"Fuck yeah. You guys make everything so expensive she can't get a job that'll pay rent." *Even in Federal Way, where nobody lives unless they have to.*

"I don't make the market, I just work in it. People pay what housing's worth. Always been that way, always will. We've got people moving here all the time, hundreds every month. Tech guys, finance industry, Amazon. People need houses. I just sell 'em."

"Yeah. A million bucks for nothin'."

"I don't make the market, I—"

"—you work in it. And if you got a plain job you're shit out of luck."

Ortega stares at Eudy. With this ski mask all he can see is my eyes, Eudy thinks. But I can see all of him. Again Ortega's fingers twitch around the bat handle. Then he looks from side to side. What's he looking for? The cops he called? Nah. He never called the cops. He grabbed the bat and ran down to play Superman, figuring that someone else would hear the crash and dial 911. Now he's stuck.

"You gonna use that?" says Eudy. "You gonna beat me up?" He steps forward. "Let's do this!"

"Stay back!"

"So where are the cops?"

"They're comin'."

"They're takin' their time."

"You make me sick. This place'd be nice if you people..."

"*Us* people?" Eudy lets that hang there for a minute, then continues. "All right. What do you make when you sell a house?"

"You mean commission?"

Eudy nods.

"Three percent."

"So what's that in money?"

Ortega's gaze shifts from Eudy to the street, and back again. He's wondering if I'm up to something, doesn't know whether to answer or not.

Finally: "Around twenty-two, twenty-five grand, usually. Sometimes more. Can be twice that."

"For one house."

Ortega nods.

"Shit, my mom doesn't make that in a year."

"I'm not your mom."

"Watch it, man." Eudy steps forward again.

"*You* watch it. I've got *this*." Ortega cocks his head toward the bat, but Eudy doesn't follow his gaze. He keeps his hazel eyes locked on Ortega's brown ones, doesn't look away, even when they hear a siren flare up in the distance.

The wail gets closer. A smile crosses Ortega's lips.

Eudy tenses, subtly shifts his weight to his back foot, ready to spring at Ortega just to get past him.

The siren swells some more, then fades, along with Ortega's smile.

Eudy decides not to smile. "Maybe somethin' big is goin' down somewhere," he says.

"They'll come."

Get him talking, distracted, Eudy thinks. Keep his mind full of stuff so he can't concentrate.

"So why is this place so expensive? Why's rent so high?"

"Lack of supply."

"Why don't they build more?"

"Ask ' em."

"I'm asking you."

"I don't care."

"That's for sure."

"Watch it!" He resets his grip on the bat.

"*Me* watch it? I gotta *respect* you too? You don't give a shit about anything but yourself."

"Says the guy who destroys a business and steals their cash. Look what you've done."

Keep his mind busy. Wait till he's not expecting it. "So why can't we find an apartment around here?"

"They've got 'em."

"Sure, two grand a month for nothing? I told you what my mom makes."

"I don't do apartments."

"You see 'em, though."

"Not much, where I am. And I got no problem with that."

"What?"

"They screw everything up. Apartments bring lots of people, noise, it messes up parking for everyone."

"Parking...?" Now he's got my mind off what I'm doing. Got to be careful. I'm probably faster than him but I have to get by him first. Concentrate.

"If you're smart you'll get yourself a career, earn money, save, and buy a house. Invest in the neighborhood, in Seattle. Invest in the American Dream. Not like these apartment people. They're trash. That's why no one wants 'em."

Now Eudy's fingers twitch. "The apartments? Or the people?"

"Both. They tried to put some on my block in West Seattle. It just means more trash like you movin' in. We stopped it good."

Eudy makes another pass with his eyes along the floor, looking for a weapon. The tipped-over snack racks are light and useless. He could grab a few cans and chuck them, but the guy looks agile. *I could find a bottle to hit him with, but that's risky. They're all plastic anyway.*

"So you're sayin' you're the reason no one can get ahead," Eudy says.

"Me? You gotta be shittin' me."

"You do it. You keep supply down. I read about it. You do this shit to your own city to protect your profits."

"You can read?"

"Yeah, I can read."

Again they stare each other down. But now Eudy is doing it to keep the man's attention away from something in the shadows beyond him.

"So you tell me," Eudy continues, "how's a guy with a plain job supposed to make it when you keep jacking up the prices?"

"I don't care about that. I care that you turn Seattle into a shithole!"

He's mad now, Eudy thinks. *One more minute.* "We don't have no choice," he says. "You have the choice. You have the power. You jack up house prices and rents, so we're fucked no matter what. Then you bitch that we're turning the place to shit. It's you, not us."

Ortega chuckles and shakes his head. "You're pissed because you're robbing stores and you're no good at it. So who do you blame? Yourself? Your mom with her plain job, her dead-end job? Don't you know? Jobs don't make it, not in Seattle. You need a *career.* But you'd rather blame the guy who's..."

A sharp *thwack!* and Ortega folds to his knees, then onto his face on the floor. Behind him Gullick stands with the crowbar from Eudy's Silverado, parked a couple of blocks away. The plan was to shift the ATM to his truck and leave the Ford to the cops.

"Go!" shouts Eudy.

"Is he gonna get up?" Gullick stares at Ortega, now collapsed on the shop floor, arms around his head where the bar struck him. As if to answer, the man lets out a slight groan and starts to prop himself up on his elbows. Slowly, but the bastard is alive.

Back in the truck, masks ripped off, cruising down Ambaum toward 518, they catch their breath and say little. Sometimes it goes like this, Eudy knows. Thanks to his planning they won't get busted. The truck owner and the shop owner will rake in their insurance and move on. The cops will take statements, but there's not much they can do. No evidence, nothing to trace. Eudy bought the chain with cash at a local hardware place in Puyallup during a busy lunch hour. He wore sunglasses and a cap—no way he'd send Gullick under a surveillance camera with that red hair.

He drops Gullick off and is home by four, and sleep finally comes after sunrise. In the early afternoon, when he rises, his mom is at the pet store. Gullick, who's just fifteen, is probably on his skateboard somewhere.

Eudy's younger brother is home, though, a copy of *HVAC Testing and Balancing* open on his lap.

"My man!" says Eudy. "Whassup?"

"Same old," says Tyler, but he smiles. He's only got a few months left and he'll be an entry-level maintenance tech. Then, with a couple of years under his belt, he'll be pulling forty, forty-five an hour, plus health insurance. Not bad. Tuition courtesy of two ATMs that Eudy had yanked up and gutted like Alki Beach clams. But Tyler doesn't know that, of course. No one does but Gullick. The guy before Gullick knew too. His name was Dom and last month his sister found him lying on her sofa overcooked on fentanyl.

Eudy pushes the foam pad he's been sleeping on against the bare living room wall to make space; Tyler gets the bedroom because he needs to study. A cup of black coffee in hand, he fires up his own laptop and checks the site of the same community college Tyler attends. He scrolls down the alphabet. *Aviation, Business, Computer Science, Electronics, Geology, Marketing...*

He stops at R, clicks on the contact form and types in *Ivan Eudy*, adds his DOB, email, phone, and the class he wants to enroll in. *Real Estate—Degrees and Certificates.*

The guy was right. Eudy isn't that good at what he does. Good enough for one more job, which he'll need for the five grand or so that tuition costs.

But in the end, jobs don't make it, not in Seattle. You need a career.

ᛉᛉᛉ

A BAD PLACE TO DIE
John Bosworth

E rik spent a half hour at Lake Union Park watching sea
planes land, and then walked south on Westlake Avenue
just after five, falling into the slipstream of employees spilling
out of their buildings toward home or in search of an after-
work happy hour.

A large man, he felt conspicuous in the white-collar crowd
and took a hunched seat at an outdoor café. He removed a
laptop from his bag, placed it on the table, and scrolled through
a news site, a practiced expression of bland neutrality on his
face.

This provided the best possible camouflage. A man in his
mid-thirties wearing a button-down shirt and staring at a
MacBook was as notable as a mailbox or lamppost. After a
moment he gradually shifted his gaze an imperceptible inch
upwards, just above the bezel of the laptop screen. Plastic ID
badges clipped to the belts and lanyards of passing employees
fell into his eyeline. Dog tags in the war for productivity, the
stream of names and pictures passing at eye level allowed him
to scan every face in the crowd without calling attention to
himself.

One of the pictures carried a promising likeness to Dean
Hamlin. He glanced up at the face, but it was a false positive
and the person—a fit, thirtyish man with a slighter chin and

143

thinner hair than his quarry—met Erik's upturned gaze, forcing his eyes back down to the laptop.

The top story on the screen concerned an orca in the Puget Sound who was carrying her dead baby afloat in an evident demonstration of grief. Interest in the story had picked up with each passing day over the previous two weeks, and now held a share of global attention. No matter who you are in the world, eventually you will relate to having had and lost something that cannot be recovered.

A pang of feeling hit Erik, and then he felt foolish. The animal kingdom in the news was a sign of domestic tranquility, after all. Go look up the front page of any newspaper from September 12, 2001, or December 8, 1941. You won't find that any moody fish made it above the fold.

The news on the next page informed him that the local population was up, wages were up, housing was up, and stock prices were up. Someone was sleeping in the bus shelter in front of the café, and the workers took a wide step to avoid the legs stretched across the pavement. You always see an uptick in people choosing to live *al fresco* when the economy is really booming.

He ordered a local IPA from an indifferent waitress and was about to turn his attention back to the door badges when he saw Dean Hamlin, for certain this time, exit the office across the street and turn briskly south, away from him.

☂

"This guy is going to be squirrely," Dash had said when he showed him the file. "Once you find him, don't let him get away from you. OK?"

Dash said "OK?" to let you know he was done speaking. He never gave the impression of wanting to know if you were in fact OK with what he had said.

"For what you take as a finder's fee," Erik said, "I was hoping for more useful insight than 'don't let him get away'."

"His name is Dean Hamlin. Desk jockey by day and weekend warrior when he's not at the office. Ultrarunner. Triathlons. CrossFit. That type of stuff. A real Captain America type. You're not going to want to spend too much time grappling with him, OK?"

The man in the picture was smiling. He had small, light blue eyes sunbaked into crow's feet and his square jaw connected straight down into a wide neck. He had what would pass in Seattle for a deep tan and carried almost no subcutaneous fat, making his exterior an anatomy lesson in sinew and tendon. The veins on his neck stood out like cables, and Erik could almost hear them thrumming with blood. It was a professional habit: when he looked at someone he saw a series of systems, structures, and hydraulics, each with its own pressure and failure points.

"You wouldn't have much luck waiting for him to keel over with a coronary," Erik said. "So who's in a hurry?"

They stood shoulder to shoulder on the high bluffs of Fort Ebey State Park, a few hours north of Seattle by ferry on Whidbey Island, looking west toward the gray-blue water of the Salish Sea.

"His employer."

"And what type of business has he gotten himself into that his employer wants someone like me to administer the health plan?"

"Warehouses and logistics, among other things."

Erik didn't say anything.

"The thing is, they find themselves facing a lawsuit about their working conditions. It's their fifth such lawsuit, in fact."

"It's a hard job," Erik said.

"It is. And made harder still when there is a digital thumb on the scale. You see, each worker in the warehouse wears a device on their arm. It buzzes your wrist if you lean in a position that's bad for your back. It buzzes if you're taking too long to pack a box. It buzzes when your shift is over. Real Big Brother stuff."

Erik knew almost nothing about Dash's life, but he had picked up little glimpses of his personality that suggested a history. He was ex-military, Erik guessed, with the trademark contempt for authority, particularly government, that bordered on paranoia. He now lived somewhere remote, he thought. Maybe in a cabin near the mountains, with solar panels and rainwater irrigation, growing his own food. No matter what your political affiliation, go far enough toward either extreme and you'll eventually find yourself with chickens and an organic garden. It's where we all meet back on the other side.

Dash flicked the photo of Hamlin. "Anyway, our man here was at work one day and stumbled across a line in the computer code of this the device. The line adds a few micro-seconds to each item they pack, making their workday longer, but not noticeably so. This makes the whole operation something like zero-point-zero-zero-five-percent more efficient, keeping the price of your dog food and coffee makers down."

Erik thought it over.

"Doesn't anyone notice that they clock in at nine a.m. and their shift ends at five-oh-three p.m.? All that added time has to go somewhere."

"Indeed it does. And where it goes, according to Dean Hamlin, is smack into their legally required fifteen-minute breaks, which are helpfully tracked on the same device. Or *fourteen-*minute breaks, I should say."

"And they're worried Hamlin will go public with it?"

"It's worse than that. He already has, in a way. He has been collecting evidence on the sly and turning it over to federal officials. They just found out."

"This evidence he gave them is pretty damning?"

"It sounds like it. Before, they could have just said *Oh, what an unfortunate mistake, somebody put a zero where there should be a one in the matrix. So sorry. Won't happen again.*"

Dash continued, "This is different. Evidently Hamlin's testimony is the smoking gun. Proof that what they're doing is intentional, which I guess is an important legal distinction. It was 'willful,' is the term. And now somebody's about to go to jail."

"And somebody really doesn't want to. Which is why we are now involved."

"That's right. And here's another thing: Hamlin doesn't know that they know. He's been acting like employee of the month, all the while funneling information back to the feds. Meanwhile they've picked up on the fact that he's the rat, and someone is really not pleased, OK?"

"So where do we come in on this?"

"The word I received is that he has a meetup with their legal defense team tonight, and that's when they want you to pick him up."

"Where's the meeting?"

"That I don't know. Go earn some of your money. He's at work right now."

"All right" Erik took the file and leafed through it.

"And you're sure you want this one? I know local work is usually not preferred, but they don't have time to import somebody, and they are paying accordingly, OK?"

"It will be fine. During the workday that whole area is mostly recent California tech transplants or H-1B visas. I'm not very likely to see anyone I went to elementary school with."

The massive hazard pay made it worth it to Erik, but any risk to their anonymity was usually a nonstarter. They didn't even know each other's real names. Dash called him Erik, as in "Erik the Red," because he usually ended a job with some colorful splashes of exsanguination as a calling card.

Erik called him "Dash" because the first time they met had been in Dash Point State Park, and Erik had to spend forty-five minutes hiking around the place to find him. Dash picked the meeting locations, and every one was in a different park or nature area around the region.

"Maybe next time I pick the meeting place," Erik said.

Dash looked out over the bluffs toward the glimmering Strait of Juan de Fuca, and the brilliant white sunlight bouncing off the snow on the Olympic Mountains to the south.

"Where would you rather be?"

"If I have to be in South Lake Union by five, I'd rather be on the ferry back."

"Well then you'd better hurry, OK?"

☂

Hamlin, the "real Captain America type," had slipped into the after-work crowd as Erik followed. Lost in a shifting array of computer bags and business casual, he didn't see anyone in blue tights.

He spotted Hamlin down the block, then lost him again, and repeated that sequence maybe five times, moving fast, trying to make up ground at the brisk walking speed of a triathlete without actually breaking into a run.

Erik was covered in a light sweat by the time Hamlin ducked into the light rail station at Westlake, and he was grateful for the break in the action.

He loitered at the end of the southbound platform until Hamlin boarded, then found a standing spot in the crowded car behind him.

The car lurched forward. "You're on the One Line," a woman's voice helpfully announced from the overhead speakers. While technically accurate, this statement was a meaningless bit of civic aspiration. A decade after the ribbon cutting on the first rail stations, the whole system still had only one line in total. The lie was only in the inflection, Erik thought. She could have said, "You're on the one line." As in, the one and only.

At Pioneer Square station, Hamlin exited with Erik close

behind, walked two blocks west on Yesler, then turned onto First Avenue and ducked into the doorway of a bar-restaurant with a black-and-white awning and a French name.

Knowing better than to follow him inside immediately, Erik walked past the restaurant and took a looping ten-minute walk down First and back again, weaving through the crosstown grid. In Occidental Square, a woman sitting cross-legged on the flagstones was selling a pile of stolen clothing. She waved an item at him, and Erik wondered if she thought he'd look good in a fuchsia Target sweater with the plastic security tag still clipped to it.

At Washington Street, an ageless form in a hooded sweat-shirt stood motionless in a fentanyl nod, completely folded over at the waist, a marionette with half of his strings cut.

Things were looking more polished in the restaurant when he entered. Overhead Edison bulbs were sparingly hung around a tastefully underlit dining room of dark wood and black metal fixtures, with an off-white granite bar running along the east wall. A man dressed all in black behind the host station performed his dual function of concierge and bouncer, a border agent protecting the place from outside threats to the ambiance. After a moment of hesitation, he allowed Erik entry to the bar area.

Erik spotted Hamlin at a table with two others in the far corner of the dining room and he took a barstool with his back to them, watching the mirrored wall behind the liquor bottles.

The bartender, a short, plump man in his early forties, expertly shook two whiskey sours with perfectly frothed egg-white tops into etched old-fashioned glasses.

Erik indicated that he would take one as well, and had two of them over the following hour, watching the interesting dynamic playing out as Hamlin sat with the lawyers. They knew he'd turned on them, but he didn't know that they knew.

Erik watched Hamlin speak, pretending to be helpful, and the lawyers smiling and nodding. But he could see it in the way they didn't fully meet Hamlin's eyes after he made certain comments, and a near-invisible contempt simmering behind their smiles.

Erik took professional stock of the room. He saw a steak knife gleaming on a service tray within reach, and a wood-handled steel corkscrew even closer. After the second drink, he started calculating the mental geometry of the angle you would want to lift someone over the second-floor balcony to maximize the odds of them landing on their neck. There was opportunity everywhere.

He turned his attention back to the table. The two lawyers— one man and one woman—were paying the check. Hamlin made a joke and they both laughed.

The woman was very pretty. Chestnut brown, shoulder-length hair, lively dark eyes, perfect white teeth, and a radiant smile. As she ducked to return her card to her bag, the mask slipped for just a fraction of a second and he saw behind it a white-hot rage. He had the sudden certain realization that he was looking at his client.

He had assumed this job was pure corporate skullduggery, sanctioned by some grimacing bald gargoyle in the C-suite, but this looked more personal.

He had watched her for the past hour and had formed a picture of her. She was small and came off as friendly. Because of that, she was easily underestimated. Likely top of her graduating class, then onto a top law school, Yale or Harvard, or Stanford if she wanted to be on the West Coast. She had moved from one rung to another in life, winning and winning again, until she didn't have to think much about what it would take to keep going. Maybe she could not abide this whistle-blower sitting across from her, eating her food, making bad jokes, about to fuck up her winning streak.

Or maybe it was pragmatic. Win this case and earn a massively lucrative promotion. Or, hell, quit and go private and keep all future billings for herself.

Maybe she really didn't like being lied to.

Or, maybe, she just didn't really mind killing people, and would have found an outlet for that impulse regardless of career.

Erik motioned the bartender over.

"Another one?"

"These are fantastic, but what I'd really like is some information. I have been sitting here for the past hour, and I am finding that cannot take my eyes of that woman over there."

The bartender smiled.

"Sure. Her name is Luongo. Lisa Luongo. She's in here all the time, always for what look like work meetings, always pays with her corporate card."

"Anything else you can tell me about her?"

"Not really. I think she's a lawyer. Sometimes I get the sense that they are negotiating over there, and I also get the sense that she always wins."

"Very interesting," Erik said, placing five twenties on the bar top.

The bartender laughed. "Best of luck, buddy, but be careful. She's a real killer."

"If you say so."

Erik felt a bit of pity for Hamlin, who suddenly seemed ridiculous, sitting at that table thinking he was getting away with something, and being completely outclassed the whole time.

The kitchen door swung open for a moment as a waiter passed through, and Erik saw a busboy hunched over, carrying a heavy-looking rack of steaming plates from the dishwasher. From there his mind jumped to the warehouse employees that Hamlin was trying to help, spending their days stooped or reaching, straining their backs and joints, afraid to get a drink or take a break. Long days. Even longer than they knew.

When Erik came back to reality, Hamlin was outside climbing into an Uber home to his wife. He had entirely missed his window to follow him out.

☂

At home, Erik was restless. A lapse like he had just experienced was not just rare, it simply did not happen.

He poured a drink and turned on the news, catching the last few seconds of the daily orca update. Sixteen days and counting.

The anchor smilingly announced the results of a survey of local residents. The majority of respondents agreed that "the tech industry has been positive for the region."

"Some good news there," the anchor said. "A rising tide lifts all boats."

Erik could not help thinking that asking a population now dominated by industry transplants what they thought of themselves was more than a little funny. A bit like asking the Nazis, after occupying France, how they were enjoying the croissants.

Uh…Gut, sehr gut. Danke.

The "rising tide" of the past decade was functioning more like a flash flood. The water level was higher today, but a lot of the original boats were flushed out of the harbor by the influx of labor and capital, replaced by newer ones.

Erik turned off the set, feeling no closer to sleep.

He took a seat at his desk and opened a window in a traceless relay browser. He spent the next hour digging for online dirt on Dean Hamlin.

Through various back channels he had access to not only archived news stories and community notices, but to full criminal records, even those that had been expunged. Part of his process was getting a vivid picture of a subject at an unflattering angle. Be it a DUI stop from twenty years ago, a child-luring complaint, or a particularly obnoxious LinkedIn post, it was never difficult to gin up some animus on a given subject. There is always at least one reason to hate someone if you are looking for it.

But at the end of the hour all he had found was that Dean Hamlin, born and raised in Seattle and a father of two, was virtually spotless. He had found only one item for his trouble: a write-up in an elementary school flyer about Hamlin reading to children in the after-school program. In the picture above the text he looked, to Erik, a little pompous.

Erik closed the browser, turned off the computer, poured another drink. He sat in the dark with a growing headache for five minutes, and then ten.

He turned the light back on, reopened the traceless browser.

Looking down, he realized he had typed *Lisa Luongo* into the search box.

☂

The following day was a Saturday, and Hamlin spent the morning at home. Just before ten, Erik watched as he exited the front door of his house in running gear and returned just under an hour later, for a quick shower and change before his final prep meeting with the lawyers.

When Hamlin slid into a booth at Emmerson's Oyster Bar on the waterfront thirty minutes later, Erik wasted no time in joining him on the opposite bench.

"Excuse me," Hamlin said, a little stiffly. "I'm here to meet someone."

"I know exactly who you are here to meet," Erik said. "The question, Mr. Hamlin, is: do you?"

Hamlin, already bracing for a very unusual day, was easily thrown. "What is that supposed to mean?"

"I can tell you exactly what it means," Erik said.

Hamlin listened without interruption, and five minutes later he was staring down at his congealing cup of salmon chowder without appetite.

"So, you've been hired to kill me."

"That's right."

"And that's what you've come here to do now."

"No, that's wrong."

Hamlin looked hopelessly disoriented. "Then what is it exactly that you want from me?"

"I want you as my *client*. I want you take over my contract, move it from your head to that of Lisa Luongo, and in doing so solve both of our problems."

Hamlin shook his head. "Oh, I couldn't do that."

"Do what?"

"Kill someone. I just couldn't do it. I'm against it on principle."

"Principle? Who gives a shit? She is going to kill you. She's from California, for christsakes."

Hamlin shrugged.

"I don't believe this. I came here to save you."

"Yes, from *you*."

"Listen, Hamlin. If it wasn't me, it would be someone else."

Hamlin thought for a moment.

"You said it would solve both of our problems. My problem is obvious. What's *your* problem?"

"My problem is simple: I don't want to kill you. Are you really too principled to join me in that goal?"

"I don't kill people," Hamlin said fixedly.

"In about twenty minutes she's going to walk through that front door with her buddy, and either way I am going to walk out the back. Really think about what tomorrow looks like for you if you don't take this deal."

"At least my family will be provided for," Hamlin said weakly. "I've saved."

"You saved for Uncle Sam, and he is grateful. There is a saying that Washington state is a good place to live and a bad place to die, because the estate tax here is so high. So you can take all that you've saved, and then cut it in half."

Erik held up a napkin and tore it down the middle.

"Your wife will sell the house just to cover the tax bill on it. She can take what's left over to a nice little townhouse in a so-so school district. Sure, she will have to scramble back to work just to keep the lights on in that cracker box, but with enough luck she'll be able to send one of your kids to college. Which one do you think she'll pick?"

"They weren't really going to kill me, right?" Hamlin said, sounding panicked.

Erik looked at the time.

"I'm sorry, we don't have time for denial. This is bargaining."

"Those lawsuits are going to continue without me. I was just helping. What would killing me guarantee them in the long term?"

"In the *long* term?" Erik asked. "Hamlin, do you know what liquefaction is?"

"What? Uh, no."

"Say you are a captain of industry and you have set up your thriving little tech company right here down the street." Hamlin indicated Alaskan Way, running behind them along the waterfront. "Liquefaction means that your MacBooks, and your Teslas, and, less alarmingly, all of your employees, are going to show up to work one fine morning and find themselves at the bottom of Puget Sound by lunchtime.

"This whole city is made up of internet-based businesses that could be run from literally anywhere on the planet, and these people chose to build them on loose soil spread over a tectonic fault line that is overdue to blow. They are not people who are thinking long-term. Somebody sees a chance to make Monday's hearing a little better for themselves, and they are taking it. So why won't you?"

Hamlin sat silent for nearly a full minute.

"All right," he said finally.

†

155

Monday would have been the first day of the preliminary hearing, which was postponed due to the tragic development.

Erik met Dash at another of his hand-picked locations, just off a trailhead in timberland on the Olympic Peninsula. They began to walk together into the forest.

After a while, Dash said, "This is not exactly what I expected from Erik the Red."

Erik shrugged.

"Have you ever used that particular method before?"

"Nope."

"Does it have a name?"

"Saxitoxin."

"What?"

"Also known as paralytic shellfish poisoning."

"You're kidding," Dash said.

Erik shook his head.

"Yeesh. Sounds like a real nasty way to die."

"Not really. Just a little tingling and numbness before you freeze up and lose consciousness. Kind of like going to sleep."

"Incredible. This is one for the scrapbook."

He handed Erik a small clipped item from that day's paper, only a few inches long: Seattle Man Dies on Light Rail. "A light rail passenger died in a north-bound car Saturday afternoon. Dean Hamlin, 37, was found unresponsive at the Northgate station..." It went on for a paragraph or two, offering few details.

"Northgate? So, he made it all the way to the end of the line before they found him," Erik said.

He wasn't really surprised. There was a term for the region's cool disinterest in other people: the Seattle Freeze. Once Hamlin made it onto the train, he was almost certain to be ignored while he seized up and stopped breathing in his seat.

Sitting there quietly, he could have ridden unbothered up and down the one line all day long if a fare enforcement officer hadn't tried to wake him for proof of payment.

"You know I'm glad this worked out," Dash said. "Some people get a little weird doing this kind of work so close to their home. They can lose perspective."

"It went very well," Erik said quickly. "No hesitation at all."

T

And it had gone well, for at least a few minutes after Hamlin accepted his offer. Erik ordered a round of Kumamoto oysters to celebrate, awash in the generous feeling of someone having his cake and eating it, too.

Then Hamlin excused himself to the restroom. Erik found himself alone with his thoughts.

And what *was* he thinking, really? Hamlin was now the only person in the world besides Dash who could identify his face, and Erik didn't even really know anything about him. In fact, the only thing he *did* know for sure about Hamlin was that he screwed over his last professional partner.

And who the hell did this guy think he was, anyway? Making Erik practically beg for the privilege of saving his life. For all he knew, Hamlin was in the bathroom testing the wire on a hidden microphone, all excited to tell the feds that he had snared them a two-for-one deal today.

And here Erik was, risking everything to screw over a client who had done him no wrong, who had offered good money, and who might offer repeat business if Erik could manage to scrounge up even the slightest amount of professionalism. He lightly touched the pocket that held the vial of saxitoxin he had brought for Lisa Luongo.

Hamlin returned to the table a few minutes later to find a fresh tray of oysters resting on ice chips.

"Olympias," Erik said. "Small in size, but big in flavor."

He handed one to Hamlin, and ate one himself.

"It tastes like copper," Hamlin said.

"Great minerality," Erik said. "Like tasting the ocean."

He picked up another and raised it, indicating Hamlin to do the same.

"To the good guys," Erik said, and tossed it back.

☂

"Why this change in tactic?" Dash asked. "Your calling card is usually a bit more spatter. You know," he waved his hands in the air, "kind of Jackson Pollock-y, OK?"

"Staying local carries enough risk without my dropping a calling card."

"It sure sounds like a better way to go out. Just drop off to sleep. There's some mercy in it."

Erik said, "I read once that *mercy* and *mercenary* both come from the Latin word for 'reward.'"

Dash looked at him.

"So now Dean Hamlin has gone onto his, and I await mine."

"Ah, right." Dash handed him an envelope. Some cash, some account information. He didn't need to inspect it. He looked around at the dense walls of Doug fir and cedar around them.

"You know," Erik said, "I actually spent a summer in this area years ago, trying to make it as a logger when I was just a kid out of high school. 'Learn a trade,' my dad said, and I liked being out in nature."

"You didn't end up liking the job, though?"

"I liked it fine."

"You don't do it anymore."

"The sports complex in Seattle has been re-named Climate Pledge Arena, if you're curious how the logging industry is doing around here these days."

Dash laughed, just as everyone who heard the name laughed.

"It used to be 'learn a trade,'" Erik said. "Now it's 'learn to code.'"

"And we saw how well that worked out for Hamlin."

"Tomorrow it will be something else, and I don't much care what it will be. I have a job. It's not for everyone, but no job is. There is an ethic to it, and I do it well."

†

Erik sat on the exposed the upper deck of the ferry on the way back. A smattering of tourists were out to sight-see, but a light rain had kicked up and most riders were down in the main cabin, or waiting it out in their cars.

Looking out over the water, he thought again of the mother orca, still dragging literal dead weight through the shifting waters, unable to move on. *Better adapt fast*, he thought, *or become yet another local resident who can't hack it in a rapidly changing environment.*

He felt the weight of the envelope in his pocket and considered what it could buy him. A fresh start, if he wanted one. He could move someplace warm. A new job, or no job at all for a while. Many possibilities presented themselves, and he considered each one in turn.

The sound of the heavy metal door banging closed brought him back around. The tourists had gone below, and he was alone on the top. The rain had picked up, along with a stiff headwind. Cold rainwater ran down his neck and under his collar. He considered following the others inside, but decided against it. He had seen lots of days like this before, and the clouds would break eventually. He was sure of it.

†††

WAS IT WOODY'S?
Hal Glatzer

W ake up, mister. Are you okay?"
The old fellow reclined against the fence by the northernmost leg of the Space Needle. His hair and beard were white and needed a trim. Was he a derelict, come to the Seattle Center looking for handouts? It was just past noon. I touched his shoulder. "Have you been here...since last night?"

He blinked; stared at me. "Huh? No! Came this mornin'." He touched the back of his head. "Somebody...."

"Where do you live?"

"Idaho." He plucked an aged fedora off the grass and looked around. "Where's my guitar?"

"There's no guitar here. Did you have one when you...fell asleep."

"I wasn' sleepin'. Somebody hit me! Made off with my guitar. I need it! There's this 'Folklife Festival' here. Starts today, right? I saw in the paper. It *is* today, isn' it?"

"Yes. May twenty-sixth." Then, just in case..."Nineteen seventy-two."

"I know that!"

"Performances start at six."

The Folklife Festival was a new event for Seattle, over the long Memorial Day weekend. What he'd probably read was a preview piece from a month ago in the *Post-Intelligencer*. I'd been interviewed for it.

"Do I have t' audition?"

"We only held auditions for bands. They'll get the big stages. But anybody can sign up for a half-hour slot on the smaller stages and…do their thing. Have you ever played in public?"

"Since before you were born!"

"Okay." I was thirty-five, and he looked to be in his sixties.

He dug into a pocket of his too-large suit jacket, and handed me two newspaper clippings. One was the *P-I* article in which I was quoted. The other was from the *Press*, in Coeur d'Alene, Idaho, dated May 12. The headline "Woody Guthrie" Lives! topped a photo of the old man on a park bench playing guitar for a handful of onlookers. His hat was on the ground, open for tips. The caption read: *Local man performs Woody Guthrie's songs on what he says is the famous folksinger's own guitar.*

Before I could ask if maybe he thought he *was* Woody Guthrie, he said, "Woody's gone now. Five years. I'm carryin' on his legacy." He tapped the guitar in the photo. "An' that was Woody's git-box. He gave it t' me."

A steel-string Gibson with a black-and-yellow sunburst finish, it did look like a guitar that Woody had been photographed with during World War II, singing pro-labor and anti-fascist songs for workers in defense plants, shipyards and aircraft factories. Many of those workers had mounted a popular, patriotic slogan on their tools, cranes, lathes and drill presses. So Woody stuck a white signboard onto his guitar and painted that same slogan on it: *This Machine Kills Fascists.*

My wife and I live in Seattle, and we don't take the Idaho papers. But if we'd seen that photo we'd have tried to get in touch with the fellow. We're officers of the non-profit Seattle Folklore Society. We know musicians all over the Northwest, and we produce concerts. That's why the National Park Service and the Smithsonian tapped the Folklore Society to launch this new Folklife Festival. The city liked the idea and offered us the Seattle Center grounds, which hadn't been used much since the

World's Fair ten years ago.

He tugged my sleeve. "You thinkin' it was never Woody's? That anybody could stick a sign like that on an ol' git-box? Help me up."

I got him under his left arm and lifted. He wasn't heavy. His gray wool suit and white shirt were clean but long out of fashion; likely they'd come from a bin in a flophouse down by Pioneer Square.

"Was it in a case?"

He snorted. "Who can afford a case? It's in my ol' duffel bag, padded with the rest o' my clothes. The only way t' carry it—to hide it—when you're sharin' a boxcar with tramps an' hoodlums."

"You rode here from Idaho on a freight train? I didn't think guys could do that anymore."

"Come with me, sometime. I'll show you how."

"No thanks."

"I need the duffel bag too. If the thief ain't my size, he's gonna throw all my clothes away."

"Where did you get the guitar?"

"Told you. Woody gave it t' me."

"You knew him? That well?"

"Yeah. Met him here in Washin'ton, on the Columbia River, back in forty-one. I got work pourin' concrete for the Gran' Coolee Dam. The Bonneville Power Authority hired Woody t' write songs about the river an' the power dams an'"—he mimicked Guthrie's voice—"the 'ee-lek-tricity.' You know about those songs?"

Like most folkies in the Northwest, I grew up singing them. "Oh, yes."

"I'd worked my way there from California with a guitar, singin' cowboy songs an' playin' for square dances. That's how Woody and me got t' be friends. We jammed an' sang t'gether, nights, while he was in the Gran' Coulee. Made a big impression on me. I've been singin' his songs ever since. That's why I rode over here. To come to this Folklife Festival an' sing Woody's Columbia River songs."

"That'd be great. We'll find a stage for you. And you're welcome to use *my* guitar."

He clutched my arm. "It wouldn' be the same if I wasn' playin' *his!*"

"Of course. We have volunteers. I'll ask them to look for it. How did you come to have...his guitar?"

"Well, I knocked aroun' after the war. Got busted singin' in a rally for some blacklisted writers."

"Arrested for *singing*?"

"For fightin' back! Punched a cop. Got sent up for assault. Finally made it t' New York when Woody was livin' in Brooklyn. Turned out we'd both served in the Merchant Marine. But *my* guitar drowned when my Liberty Ship got torpedoed. Woody had...I don' know: five or six guitars. So he said, 'Take one o' mine.' He was that kinda guy. You play too, I guess."

"My wife and I are in an old-timey string band. She's a fiddler. My name's Phil."

"Carl." We shook hands.

"Do you want a cup of coffee or anything?"

"Got someplace I can...wash up?"

"Sure." I led him across the lawn to the Armory building, our headquarters for the Festival, and pointed him to the men's room.

I walked the opposite way down the hall, to the supply closet we were using as the lost-and-found repository. Alongside a rucksack and three umbrellas, there was a war-surplus duffel bag. I looked inside; saw men's clothes but no guitar. Was it Carl's? He'd have to say so before I took it out.

On the stairway up, one of my wife's fiddle students hailed me: a teenager named Barbara who, because she played the old-timey style, called herself "Granny" on stage. "Hey, Phil. Is anybody selling strings yet?"

"All the vendors for instruments and music merchandise are

in a white tent over by the Food Circus stage."

"Thanks."

"They should be through setting up their booths by now. When you get there, tell everyone to keep an eye out for a guitar that might be stolen." I described it to her.

"'Fascists?'"

"If it really belonged to Woody, it's a piece of American history."

I trotted upstairs. Just as I reached the door of the Festival office, a man inside was yelling, "You gonna let that Commie sing those pinko songs?" He was elderly but heavyset, looming over my wife at her desk.

I stepped in quickly. I was close enough to his size to cool his choler. "Excuse me. Can I help you?"

"This gentleman," she said, "feels that one of our performers ought not to have a stage. But—as I told you, sir—we don't have that name on our roster. Are *you* one of our scheduled performers?"

"No. But—"

"How do you do, sir. I'm Phil. This is Vivian. We're in charge of the Festival."

On his florid face, the right cheek twitched as we shook hands. "Richard."

"Where are you from, Richard?"

"Idaho."

Vivian smiled. "Welcome to Seattle. We have several participants here from Idaho. Do you compete in the old-time fiddling contest in Weiser?"

"Are you one of the Basque dancers from Boise?"

"No. I'm a preacher. My church is in the Idaho panhandle. Me and some of my congregation came over here to protest the inclusion of Communists in your festival. One in particular, like I said. Back in Idaho, he sings Red songs. Woody Guthrie songs."

"Oh. I know who you mean."

The tic in his cheek fluttered again. "Guthrie's a notorious

Commie. And this pinko's un-American. Un-patriotic!"

"He's a veteran."

"So am I!"

"Look, Richard. The Folklife Festival is open to anybody who signs up. Dancers and singers from a dozen ethnic traditions are coming from all over the Northwest: from Idaho to Puget Sound, Oregon to B.C. and Alaska."

"I bet they're *all* left-wingers!"

"I doubt that."

"Give me a pulpit to deliver an anti-Communist sermon."

Vivian said, "Are you gospel singers? We could give your church group a stage."

The tic again. "Sure. We've got hymns."

I nodded. "In that case, okay. We'll find you a half-hour time slot."

"That's white of you. Thanks." He checked his watch. "I need to get back to my boys."

"All male?"

"Huh?"

"Voices in your choir."

"Yeah. Is there a place where we can get together now? Away from other people?"

"Rehearsal space? Of course. Room one-oh-six, downstairs. What's your group called?"

"The National Church of Christ, Christian." He headed for the door.

"And you're from…where, exactly?"

He called over his shoulder, "North of Coeur d'Alene: Hayden Lake," and went out.

Vivian looked up from her clipboard. "Want to tell me about the, uh, 'pinko?'"

I slid my chair next to hers and told her.

"Richard and his congregation might heckle him."

"Can we keep them apart? Opposite ends of the grounds at the same time?"

"Not anymore! Hardly any slots are still open."

"I don't want us to get crushed between two World War II veterans."

"Speaking of war—while you were out, we got word that a group of protesters confronted some soldiers and sailors on leave from Vietnam, in one of the parking lots. When the police showed up, everybody walked away."

The possibility of trouble like that had come up in our discussions with the Smithsonian, the National Park Service, and the City. Folksingers do tend to be on the left side of politics, and some anti-war songs have been big hits on the pop charts. My being a lawyer impressed the deputy chief of police. But he told me, "We'll be here to keep the peace. If there's a riot, we'll clear *everybody* out, and shut you down."

Vivian touched my arm. "I hope that's the only such incident. If we don't have 'Peace Now,' we won't have a Festival."

I settled into my chair. "Oh. I saw Barbara. Told her about the missing guitar. I better get the word out, all around."

Seattle Civil Defense had loaned us a dozen walkie-talkies to manage the activities and deal with emergencies. I unhooked mine from my belt and touched the press-to-talk button. "Attention volunteer coordinators and stage managers. Be on the lookout for a stolen guitar." I gave its description.

Vivian paged through the venue rosters. "I can give the church group one of the small stages at two thirty Saturday afternoon. The Guthrie guy could take the same stage on Sunday at five thirty."

"Switch 'em around. Church on Sunday."

She snickered. "But still a potential for confrontation."

"We'll have to take that chance. And I can ask for a cop to be posted at both performances. Even if that choir can't sing very well, it'll be good PR for the Folklore Society. Boost our chances of putting on another Festival next year if we can show we're open to all kinds of people—not just old lefties."

"My husband, the diplomat!" She kissed me, then wrote

down the assignments in her clipboard. The office was quiet. I took a deep breath, closed my eyes....

A knock on the doorpost. I looked up. Carl made a little wave and ambled in.

"Carl—Vivian."

"Hi, Carl."

"Nice to meet you. Any word on my guitar?"

"Not yet. But come downstairs. Let's see if it's your duffel bag in the lost-and-found."

It was. He lugged it upstairs. "Can I hang out here in your office?"

"Sure." I gestured toward a chair and gave him some issues of the Folklore Society's newsletter.

Another knock at the open door.

Mark stuck his head inside. He was the most advanced of Vivian's fiddle students, and fast becoming a monster on guitar too. Though he was only eleven, he performed with the teenagers in "Granny's" band.

"Hey, Phil. There's something you gotta hear."

I followed him down to Room 106. The door was closed, muffling the sound within. But it was a call-and-response: one voice, then a chorus, in rhythm.

"That's a church group, Mark. Gospel singers."

"They're not singing. They're yelling. Like a drill sergeant with recruits."

"I guess that's their thing: fire-and-brimstone, hell-and-damnation. Some churches are like that."

"Not *my* church."

"Mine, neither. But there are all kinds of churches, Mark. We have to be tolerant of—"

"They wear uniforms."

"Huh?"

"I saw them go in with an old man. Four young guys—older than me, like soldiers' age."

"What kind of uniforms?"

"Silver-colored shirts, with a big white cross stitched on"—he tapped the breast pocket of my shirt—"right there."

I shrugged. "The Festival's open to everybody."

"Yeah, but—"

"Thank you for letting me know."

"Sure. See you later, Phil." He headed out onto the grounds.

I went back up to the office to deal with the paperwork for which Vivian and I, as the Festival's head honchos, were responsible. By two thirty I'd dealt with forms in two manila folders and had just opened a third when my walkie-talkie buzzed.

"This is Joe. I'm standing outside the instrument dealers' tent. Stu says I should tell you: that guitar you were looking for—some guy just brought it in and offered to sell it to him."

Carl jumped up. "I have t' get it back!"

"Hang on, Carl. We'll go there together."

Vivian told one of the volunteers to take charge of the office. I telephoned the Center's police line. "It's Phil. I need an officer to meet me at the white tent."

The three of us hurried downstairs and crossed the Festival grounds. The Center's gates had been open less than three hours, but admission was free, and festivalgoers were streaming in. We expected to draw fifty thousand—hopefully more—over the three-day weekend.

I told Carl, "Stu buys and sells vintage guitars. But don't worry. He won't touch hot merchandise. He posts handbills in his shop, with photos of stolen instruments from all over the country."

"Thanks for coming, Phil," said Stu as we walked into the tent. "You and Vivian have got to see this!" He and Cliff, his shop's repairman, were passing a Gibson back and forth between them, first holding it close, peering inside, then assessing it at arm's length. Cliff handed it to me.

It looked like the one Carl was playing in the Idaho newspaper photo. And it had the white sign on top, with *This Machine*

Kills Fascists in black paint.

Richard stood on one side of Stu's booth. Four crew-cut young men huddled behind him, all wearing silvery shirts with monogrammed crosses.

Carl strode over to the other end of the booth.

The tent was crowded with musicians looking to buy gear. Barbara and Mark were there. And a uniformed Seattle cop showed up right after we did. All that body heat was driving up the temperature inside.

I handed the guitar back to Stu. He inclined his head toward the teenager standing closest to Richard. "That young man brought it in."

"Yeah," said the boy. "What'll you gimme for it?"

Carl piped up. "It's not his. It belonged to Woody Guthrie. An' *he* gave it to *me*!"

Richard's cheek twitched. "Guthrie was a Commie!"

"In the war," said Carl, "Russia was our ally. Remember?"

"That was a mistake! We should've helped Hitler fight the Russians!"

One of Richard's boys said, "If America'd done that, we coulda got rid of the Jews, too!"

Another said, "Yeah. And the Blacks!"

Hubbub! From all over the tent, people were shouting them down. A few men and women edged forward.

Carl yelled, "You think you're the 'master race?'"

"The *white* race! We sure are! You're white. Be proud of it, like my son Freddy here!" He put his arm around the boy who'd brought the guitar in. Then he turned with him to face the crowd. "Join us! We're the National Church of Christ, Christian. We're *against* Communism, and *for* the white race."

"That's what the Nazis said!"

Richard stepped closer. He outweighed Carl by a hundred pounds at least. "There's plenty of white men in this country and all over the world, that feel the way we do."

Carl stood his ground. "Plenty of fascists, you mean. Franco in Spain. Peron in Argentina. Are they your heroes?"

The cop had been moving forward through the crowd, all along. "That's enough!" he announced. "Get away from each other. Both of you, take three steps back."

I raised my hands, palms out. "Everybody. Just cool it!"

Carl backed off but squinted at Richard. "I *know* you."

"What?"

"From Coeur d'Alene. You and your son heard me sing." He dug the clipping out of his pocket and held it up to show it around, pointing to two of the listeners. "That's them!" He turned to face Richard again. "An' now I remember the *first* time I saw you: in LA, before the war. You were famous! You headed up a pro-German bund called the Silver Shirts. An' those must be the shirts. They smell from mothballs!"

The crowd's laughter stung Richard. He snorted, turned to his son. "Tell them what you told me."

Freddy puffed himself up. "I'm a Commie-hunter, like my dad. We heard this Red say he was coming here to spread his propaganda. So I caught the same freight train he did, slept in the same flophouse, followed him up here this morning and...confiscated that pinko's guitar in the name of the white race."

"Knocked me out and *stole it!*" Carl raised a fist.

Stu shook his head. "Don't worry, sir. I won't buy it. Nobody will. I'll send word to every dealer and collector—"

Richard leaped over and grabbed it out of Stu's hand, elbowed people aside, ran through the open tent flap and out onto the grass. Carl tried to stop him. But two of Richard's boys pinned his arms from behind. And while a third blocked interference, Freddy caught Carl on the chin with an uppercut and a roundhouse punch to the gut that knocked the wind out of him. The cop grabbed Freddy and tried to handcuff him, but the kid wriggled free and ran outside, followed by the other goons.

Vivian and I sprinted out in pursuit. The cop radioed for

help. Four left their posts on the perimeter and ran onto the lawn.

The Center was crowded not only with festivalgoers but with clusters of rehearsing performers. Richard dodged a troupe of Scandinavian dancers only to bump into a chorus of shape-note singers, knocking two to the ground. He stumbled but recovered and kept running.

One of Richard's boys collided with a little girl clutching a balloon; he laughed as it wafted away. The girl's mother swung her umbrella against the boy's legs. He tripped and fell. A cop dashed over and handcuffed him. Another of the boys knocked down a Morris-dancer, tearing the fellow's white costume and making his ankle-bells jingle. A third boy plowed through a bluegrass band, snagging his silver shirt on the banjo's tuning pegs. Onlookers joined the performers in holding on to the bullies and handing them over to the cops.

Intrigued by all the commotion, crowds started trotting after us.

Richard ran toward the Space Needle. He was too corpulent to run fast, but he'd had a head start. There was a gap in the fence not far from where I'd found Carl earlier. Richard ducked through it and took hold of a maintenance ladder that ran up the northernmost leg of the tower. Clutching the guitar kept him from gripping the rungs. He could only slide his free hand up the side-support as he took each step up.

Vivian grabbed my arm. "Don't even think about—"

"Sorry. I've got to!" I started climbing the ladder. Vivian shrugged and followed me.

Richard surely could not make the six-hundred-foot climb to the restaurant at the summit. But he had enough stamina to reach the unfinished steel decking, only a hundred feet up, where the City had started building a sightseeing platform. The elevator makes a stop there, for the workers. But no one was working that weekend; and the decks were closed to the public anyway. There were no fences or guardrails.

Richard was wheezing when he got to a hatch at the top of the ladder. He heaved it up and open, then pushed the guitar through. Finally able to use both hands, he hoisted himself onto the narrow platform.

Vivian and I weren't athletic, but we'd managed to narrow the gap a few rungs at a time. I poked my head up through the hatch. The wind was gusting. Richard had to crouch to keep his balance as he stepped toward the edge of the platform.

"White people!" he yelled to the crowd staring up at him. "Help us return America to its roots. Make America a Christian nation!" Undaunted by the boos and catcalls from below, he added, "A *white* Christian nation!"

I got myself onto the platform and gave Vivian a hand up. The wind threatened to knock us down and sweep us off the deck. So we made our way toward Richard on all fours. He saw us, turned aside, yanked away the barrier across the elevator door and punched the call-button repeatedly.

Panting, I managed to say, "Give me the guitar, Richard."

"*Dad! Dad!*" It was Freddy, calling to him from the ground.

Richard made his way slowly in that direction, to the edge of the deck.

I lay down prone, and crab-scuttled to where I could get my head over the edge and look down.

Freddy spread his arms apart. "*Toss it to me! I'll catch it!*"

Vivian yelled, "Don't do it, Richard!"

He snarled at her. "Freddy's a wide receiver." He gauged the angle and the distance and, when the wind relaxed for a moment, hurled the guitar toward his son.

But no matter how well he might catch a football, Freddy could not gather the guitar into his arms and cushion its fall. It slammed into his face, knocked him backward onto the grass, and broke apart.

I scrambled over and grabbed Richard's arm just as the elevator arrived. Vivian clutched his other arm. We managed to wrangle him into the cab and ride down to the ground.

173

The crowd was enormous. The deputy police chief was directing uniformed officers to hold them back. Two festival volunteers were urging people to please go elsewhere.

Richard ran to where his son lay and knelt beside him. The boy's face was crushed into a bloody mess. A cop standing watch beckoned us over and whispered, "Massive head trauma. The kid's dead."

Vivian said, "Richard, I'm so sorry."

I tried to lay a gentle hand on his shoulder. But he growled, "Go away!"

We did. We backed off and wrapped ourselves in a big hug while our pumped-up adrenaline subsided.

The deputy chief touched my elbow. "I'm sorry, Phil. A fatal accident. A big crowd. It's a dangerous situation. My riot team's standing by. I'm going to close the Festival down."

"Please don't! It's terrible, what happened," said Vivian. "But it's not a riot or a confrontation. See? Nobody's making trouble. Our volunteers are working alongside your officers, getting people to go away."

I added, "Please let us help you. Give us a chance."

After a few seconds, he said, "Go ahead."

I unhooked my walkie-talkie. "This is an emergency. We need to move a bunch of people away from the north end of the Space Needle. I need more volunteers right away, to work with the police."

We stepped aside to let an ambulance drive up.

The crowd was still noisy, but three volunteers arrived and joined the line of cops herding the crowd away. The deputy chief said, "Okay, Phil." Then, into his radio, "Riot team—stand down. Everything's under control."

Carl was looking down at the pieces of the guitar. "Can it be repaired?"

I picked them up and handed them to Stu. The neck had snapped off the body but was still tethered by all six strings to the bridge. The back of the guitar was cracked open. The white signboard had come off the top.

Stu passed everything to Cliff, who said, "Yeah. And worth fixing. It's a pre-war Gibson from nineteen thirty-eight or early thirty-nine."

"We can tell," said Stu, "by the inlays on the fingerboard, the logo on the peg-head, and the serial number inside."

Carl looked at me. "Told you! Woody played it in the war."

Stu shrugged. "Well, it's old enough. But there's no way I can tell for sure that Woody actually owned it."

"He did!"

Two orderlies shifted Freddy onto a stretcher and loaded him into the ambulance. Richard and the cop got in, too. Once they'd driven away there was no more drama to hold the crowd. The last of them drifted off.

Cliff said, "I'm sorry, Carl. There *have* been forgeries. People take an old guitar and stick on a sign like this, trying to pass it off as—"

"Wait a second," said Vivian. She turned over the signboard. On the back, where it had been attached to the top, there were blobs of old, dried glue. But something had been drawn on there: a caricature of a guitar player with his head tipped all the way back and his mouth open, singing.

Carl said, "That's Woody! He drew himself like that. You see it in his letters."

"Yes!" I grinned. "It's in his songbook, too, from nineteen forty-six. We have a copy."

Vivian touched Cliff's arm. "If a forger were making a fake, why go to the trouble of drawing this cartoon and then putting it where nobody'd see it?"

Cliff said, "Okay. Looks like Woody did own the guitar. C'mon, Carl. Let's go back to the tent. Stu and I'll work out what it'll take to repair."

"Uh, how much d'you think...?"

I jumped in. "Send me the bill."

Vivian took my hand, and we started for the office together.

We'd have questions to answer from the police, the newspapers, and our performers. But the Folklife Festival would go on.

Suddenly, she stopped. "What Woody wrote on his guitar. That 'machine!' It really—"

"Don't say it!"

🌂

AUTHOR'S NOTE: *The first "Folklife Festival" in 1972 drew 123,000 attendees. Nowadays, called The Northwest Folklife Festival, and brings twice that many people to the Seattle Center every year.*

🌂🌂🌂

GO WITH THE FLOW
Bonnar Spring

A good friend will help you move,
but your best friend will help you move a body.

There's only one thing worse than having your ex-husband on your doorstep first thing in the morning. And that's finding him slumped against your front porch railing with a bullet hole in the center of his forehead.

I'm inhaling my first sips of coffee when the *beep-beep-beep* of the garbage trunk sounds in the next block. And I forgot to take out the trash last night.

Damn.

The can is overflowing. Nothing for it but to run outside and haul it to the curb, pronto. With the persistent autumn rains, dragging the can out will be a slog through puddles and waterlogged grass. I step out of my slippers and cinch my robe tighter. Open the door.

Keith?

My ex-husband is sitting on the wide boards of the porch. His back against the railing. His feet splayed. His head drooping sideways.

What the hell?

We don't have the sort of casual relationship that some people

have with their exes. In fact, Keith and I have as little relationship as possible. No kids. No pets. No alimony.

If he'd just sign the damn papers selling me the house, I'd be
happy never to see him again. There's no way Keith could've
come up with enough money to buy me out—and it was too
much of a stretch to think he'd had a change of heart. Our
shouting match at the lawyer's last Tuesday concluded with an
obscenity-filled tirade—hateful and vulgar, even for a foul-
mouthed jerk like him.

All of which begs the question of why I married him in the
first place. Chalk it up to a bad case of youthful stupidity. He
could be charming when he wanted; it's just that he stopped
wanting.

"What the fuck, Keith?" I nudge him with my bare toe when
he doesn't wake up, so distracted by the absurdity of his
presence that it takes until then to register the third eye.

A small round hole, black in the center. Puckered and red
around the edge. A line of dark red, like a trail of rusty tears,
snakes down his cheek and disappears in a fold of his neck.

My brain sputters.

He's *dead*?

Hand over mouth, my heart accelerating painfully, I take a
step toward him. I should get closer and check for a pulse, but
that hole...geez, of course he's dead.

It takes a minute for paralyzing shock to subside. My breathing calms, and I run my fingers through tangled curls. I had a
restless night, but I didn't hear a gunshot—and I certainly didn't
hear the doorbell. It rained off and on. Some thunder and
lightning. Maybe that masked the sound.

Now that I've secured financing, all Keith needed to do was
sign his name a few times, and I'd hand him enough money to
jet off into the sunset. I seriously can't imagine he felt *that*
distressed about losing the house. Anyhow, Keith's MO is all
about blaming me—or whoever's handy—for his problems.
Most of which spring from the firm belief that he deserves

whatever he wants, can do whatever he wants. And he is *always* right.

He'd never kill himself over the house. Kill *me* is far more likely.

I peer at Keith. He really could be sleeping: head tilted, hands clenched at his sides.

But where's the gun?

I scour the area, even the flower patch below the porch.

A bullet hole, but no gun. So...*someone shot him?*

I sway from foot to foot, like I have to pee. *What the fuck am I going to do?* So what if I don't own a gun? I can't call the cops. In my fit of fury outside the lawyer's office, I all but threatened to kill him for refusing to sign. They'll never believe me.

The trash truck turns the corner, stops three doors down.

Instant panic.

My dead ex-husband is on my porch, and the garbage collectors are friendly guys. I bolt down the steps to the garden gate, retrieve the can, and push it to the curb.

The truck stops two doors down. The guy hanging on the curbside door waves hello and yells, "Mornin', Jane. You're up early."

Wake the neighbors, why don't you?

I paste on a smile while I run back to the porch to block the sight lines. The truck rumbles down the street, takes a left at the corner, and disappears.

Now what?

Just get him away from here. The thought comes out of nowhere.

If I can get rid of Keith's body, there shouldn't be anything to link him with me, Well, of course, he's linked to me: he's my ex, but not, you know, *linked* as in he came back yet again to bang on my door and shout obscenities, so I'd bought a gun and shot him when he showed up.

Keith's enough of an asshole that there are probably hundreds of suspects: his bookie, that bizarre woman he's dating, his business partner who accused him of skimming...

How do I make him disappear?

Focus, Jane.

"Godammit, Keith, did you drive here? I hope to hell I don't have to go rooting around in your pants pocket for the car keys."

Whidbey Island is quiet, and my little street in the center of the island is *very* quiet, with large wooded lots. We have driveways; no one parks in the street. Still, I look up and down the road. No red Bronco. He couldn't have walked. The apartment he's renting is at least twenty miles away.

Wait. No gun. No car.

Oh, shit.

Someone must've come with Keith and left in his car—or shot him somewhere else and dumped him here. Which? I don't know much about guns, but I've watched enough TV to absorb basic stuff—like only a small pistol would make that precise hole. Quiet-ish. Meaning I wouldn't necessarily hear a shot on the porch while sleeping upstairs on a stormy night—and *couldn't* hear one if Keith's death came in an after-hours bar fight in town.

Anyhow, no matter where Keith was shot, *the killer* knows there's a dead guy on my porch. What if he calls the cops...and they come to investigate? It's only been a few minutes since I opened the door, but I don't know how much time I have.

Keith has to disappear. Like right now.

Right. he's six-two, two hundred and change. A dead weight. The laugh that burbles up—I can't help it—is one hundred percent hysterics. But I have to try. The tarp in the shed would be a good start, and when I run out to grab it, I spy my wheelbarrow against the side of the garage.

I get an out-of-body experience, like I'm watching myself approach Keith from above. I spread the tarp on the wooden boards of the porch. My breath catches. I've never touched a dead body before, and I don't want to now.

I reach out to the tiger tattoo, partially visible under his short-sleeve shirt. The skin on his upper arm is pale and cool. I push. No movement. I shove harder and Keith tips sideways onto the tarp, falling with his torso and legs bent almost ninety degrees.

I've gotten as far as imagining I'd roll him up in the tarp like a rug and lay it—him—across the wheelbarrow. Get it—him—into the van and *away*. I bend down to extend his legs, but they don't budge. The words "rigor mortis" float into my mind. He's not going to straighten out, not any time soon.

I can't make a neat cigar-shaped roll with him folded like a Barbie. And I'll never be able to move an unwieldy bundle like this.

That's it. I need help, and there's only one person I can count on.

☂

But Josh answers the phone. Josh is *not* that person.

"Hey, can I speak to Amy for a sec?" I need my best friend.

"You okay?"

Obviously my voice isn't as under-control as I think. I do my instant de-stressor—a pranayama breath and affirmation: *I can do this.*

"Just frazzled. Crazy morning. I need Amy to talk me off the ledge."

Josh gets my snarky tone well enough to understand my attempt at humor, so he chuckles. "Sure. Hang on. I'll get her."

"To what do I owe the pleasure of this early-morning call?" Amy's breathless, her voice pitched high. I've either interrupted a fight with Josh or else one of their passionate reconciliations. I'm sure I'll hear all about it. As usual. Their relational drama is exhausting. Just one more reason I'm glad to be single again.

"Can you come over? Right away. I need you."

"See you in five."

That's the thing about best friends. She didn't even ask why.

I fold the tarp over Keith. That's all I can do for now to hide his body. Then I run inside to get dressed. And hope to hell Amy will help me get Keith out of here before anyone comes nosing around.

I pull on jeans, sneakers, and an old sweatshirt, and pack my tote with the professional attire I need for work. I have to make it look like a normal day, and the gallery opens in—I check the time—ninety minutes, give or take. Twenty minutes to get into town; lots of rolling woods alongside the road for the first half of the drive. I can't be the only person in the world who's looked out car windows at a vast expanse of forest bordering a road and thought, *What a great place to dump a body*. Let it roll down the hill into the woods—years might pass before a hunter or a dog walker or some dude needing to pee stops in the same spot and discovers it.

But what about all those cameras? Sneaky little CCTV things on random light poles. You see stories all the time about people getting caught somewhere they weren't supposed to be, doing something they shouldn't be doing. Even a passing car at just the wrong time could screw things up. There must be a better way.

Shit. And I'm supposed to feed my boss' cat this morning. Sarah's place is on the other side of the island. In totally the wrong direction.

Oh my god.

I run inside to check the chart I keep on the fridge. With a slight adjustment to the plan, it'll be perfect.

☂

I'm on the porch when Amy pulls into the driveway with a

flourish of spraying gravel. She bounds out of the car, eyes wide.

This is so surreal. I'm about to ask my best friend to help me move my ex-husband's body. But I don't have to. She's taking the steps two at a time before I can open my mouth. The lumpy tarp is obviously out of place. And then, it turns out there's a leather work boot protruding from the far corner.

"Holy moly!"

"It's Keith. And I didn't do it."

Amy's eyes blink like she's sending Morse code; her mouth opens to that classic big round O, but no words emerge.

"I don't know what happened to him. And I don't understand it at all, but we have to get him out of here." My voice screeches as I belt out the last part.

"But, Jane?" It's almost a whisper.

Aside from occasional promiscuous escapades, Amy's a pretty straight arrow, and I know she's going to keep grousing. "No buts."

"But you can—"

"Amy. No."

"But the police—"

"This is not up for discussion. He has to go. Now. I'm scared." She probably thinks I killed him. But playing the "I'm scared" card is the only way I know to shut down her instinctive, naïve helpfulness.

Amy bounces a curled knuckle against her mouth, quiet for a lot longer than she was on the phone when I asked her to come over. Looking down at the motionless tarp, not at me. Moving a body really is a humongous ask.

At last, she lets out a deep, deep sigh. "Okay. What can I do?"

"Help me get him into the van. We're driving over to Sarah's."

"You're going to leave him at *Sarah's*?"

"No, no." I shake my head, like a swimmer desperate to clear her ears. "Listen, we don't have time. I'll explain on the way."

This time, Amy's chin angles up, then sharply down. "All right."

We wrap the tarp as best we can around Keith's body. I bring the wheelbarrow to the foot of the steps, positioning the steel tray so the top is even with the second step. With her pulling and me pushing, we bump Keith down one step, two, and then into the wheelbarrow. Amy trundles our load across the muddy grass while I steady it.

When we reach the back of my van, I open the hatch and, with us lifting from both sides, the transition is smooth. Then I position an oblong FedEx box on top of the tarp, return the wheelbarrow to its place by the gate, and climb into the van.

"I don't know." Amy's buckling her seatbelt. "This sounds like a really bad idea. Look at the gouges in your grass. Anyone with half a brain could tell you've moved something heavy"— she rolls her eyes—"like a body across the lawn."

"Amy. Shut. Up." You can say that to best friends. "With no *body* here, nobody can prove anything." I start the engine and back down the driveway.

She shrugs, but I know she'll keep trying. "And then they'll find blood on the porch or look in your car and find material from the tarp or—"

"I've got this." I accelerate down the road. Stop at the cross street. Turn west onto Bayview Road.

We did it—well, halfway. We got Keith away from my house. I've thought about our route to Sarah's. We'll take back roads. Stick to the speed limit. With intermittent rain on an early weekday morning, there won't be much traffic—and I've never seen an Island County deputy patrolling.

The porch looked clean, but I'll take the garden hose to it when I get home. And I can stomp around in the yard. Fill the wheelbarrow with the mulch I've been meaning to spread in the front garden. Confuse the issue.

I'm still worried and, yeah, I'm probably doing a million things wrong. *But* every little thing I do to get Keith away from my front door feels like breathing room.

It's hard to face the other piece—that someone must've brought Keith to my doorstep. Someone who hated me enough to put me on the hook for a murder rap. And why would anyone who wanted Keith dead want to frame *me*—who also hated Keith?

While my eyes stay on the empty road and the speedometer, my brain works on the puzzle—yes!

I bet Keith hadn't changed his driver's license, the one with my address on it—*our* address until I threw him out six months ago. So it really could've been some random asshole who didn't know what to do with his body. So he brought Keith home—what he thought was Keith's home. Once we finish this, I'll share my ideas with Amy, so we can brainstorm.

At that thought, I almost smile for the first time since I opened my door this morning.

Now, on to step two.

Good time to change the subject. "So, what did I interrupt this morning when I called?"

Amy jumps like I've scalded her, then tosses her head and looks out the window. That's *Amy's* way of changing the subject. I still don't know if I interrupted a fight or a reconciliation this morning. So I probe.

"You still seeing that other guy?"

A quick inhale. "Well..."

"'Well' means yes, right?"

Sigh. "Mmmmm."

"You really ought to give him up, honey." I reach out to squeeze her shoulder. "I can think of a thousand better ways to get an endorphin high than banging your Pilates instructor." I turn the gentle squeeze into a mock punch. "Even if he is hot, hard as a rock, and ten years younger."

Amy probably thinks she's smiling, but I'd call it a smirk. "I'll take it under advisement."

"I can't believe Josh isn't suspicious about your having classes at such odd hours."

"I can't believe you told Keith about him." One of Amy's famous *non sequiturs*.

"Eh—" I throw my hands up until we drift into the other lane. "At this point, you're lucky the whole island doesn't know." *Time to act like a best friend.* "I really am sorry, though. It's just that Keith came home right after that time you phoned me in a panic about the close call when Josh came to the studio to surprise you for lunch and interrupted you two. I was pretty stressed out myself—and furious with you for gambling with your life that way. And I just...ended up unloading to Keith everything you said. I'm really sorry."

Amy gives me a side-eye and says, deadpan, "So, maybe it's just as well he's dead, then."

Since we've apparently hit the brick wall of *that* conversation, I tell her what I have in mind at Sarah's.

☂

Sarah owns the gallery I manage and we've become, well, not exactly friends—she writes my paycheck, after all—but friendly. We do lunch every couple of weeks, though, and I take care of her house when she's away. She's been super-helpful during my divorce, especially with this crazy house dispute. Sarah's offer of a no-strings loan was the only way I could afford to buy Keith out.

But while I love her dearly and am so grateful to her, Sarah would never get the dead-body call.

Whidbey is a long, narrow island, a few hours north and west of Seattle. Sarah's house on the west side fronts Admiralty Inlet, with serene views of Marrowstone Island and Port Townsend through a gauzy veil of gray mist. It's fifteen minutes from my place and a few million dollars out of my league. She and her newest husband are in Italy for the Venice Regatta.

We make the drive without incident—thank God—and I pull into Sarah's long driveway. Instead of parking by the back door, I roll three-quarters of the way down their boat ramp.

While the north end of Whidbey Island features dramatic high bluffs, here in Mutiny Bay Shores there's a gentle sweep to the sea. Neighbors are pretty close but Sarah's into nude sunbathing. A long time ago she planted a windbreak of Lombardy poplars on both sides of their property.

Although they have security cameras to monitor the driveway, front door, and back door, with her privacy concerns, Sarah didn't install any in the backyard patio—which leads down to their boat ramp.

It's as private as Sarah can make it, and today I'm going to take full advantage.

"Time to rock and roll," I tell Amy.

We lift Keith—still in the tarp—from trunk to tarmac and drag him to the water's edge.

According to the tide chart I keep on my fridge, high tide passed about thirty minutes ago. It's still relatively slack water, though, so we've arrived a bit early.

Admiralty Inlet forms the northern part of Puget's Sound's main basin. Nearly all the tidal seawater flowing into and out of Puget Sound passes through this narrow channel. On the ebb tide, currents reach six knots or more as water streams north past Whidbey—on to the Salish Sea and beyond, into the Pacific Ocean. And Keith's body should stream right along with it.

When we go out in Sarah's boat, she always checks the state of the tide first. Trying to go south on an ebb tide is slow and choppy. No fun for sunbathing or sipping wine coolers. On the other hand, running *with* the tide can be a thrill ride. Also not good for sunbathing or sipping. For boating, the best times are like now—slack water.

But Keith's last run needs to be bat-outta-hell fast.

I'm not sure I can stand it, but we have to wait. I go inside to feed the cat and water Sarah's fussy houseplants. Amy sits in the van. She subsided into uncharacteristic silence after I explained my plan and, by the time we got to Sarah's, her eyes drooped at half-mast, her head bowed. I only hope this wasn't too much to ask.

The water's moving faster when I return, and the waterline on the boat ramp has already receded about a foot.

Amy gets out of the van where she's huddled while I did the inside chores. She points to the steel-gray sky. "More rain coming."

Good. Rain will keep people indoors. Still, I scan the far shore of the inlet and the neighboring lots to make sure there's not some random crazy birdwatcher hoping to catch sight of a Harlequin duck. "Yep, let's go."

Amy helps me pull the tarp to the water's edge. My sneakers slosh when I nudge it into the sea. I don't want Keith to float away in my tarp. I doubt there's anything that identifies it as mine but, unlike a body that will bob along near the surface, tarps sink. If Keith is still wrapped in it when it snags on an underwater rock formation or submerged tree trunk, he might not get all the way to Japan.

At just past high tide, there should be very few places to trap him, but still...

Amy's hanging back now. I guess she feels like she's complied with the essential requirements of body moving I don't blame her. This is macabre.

I roll Keith over, close to the rushing current.

The water lifts his head. *Aaaaaaaaaahhh. Jesus.* For one long second, it looks like he's waking up. I give him another push until he's half floating. His torso bobs in the swell. His right arm sways—almost like he's waving. Again, I get that jolting *he's alive* fright.

Just one more hard push. When I do, his clenched fist gets caught in a wavelet, and there's a flash of something sparkly poking from Keith's hand. With the waves plashing at me, it's hard to see. I bend down and pull whatever it is from between his fingers.

It's a glistening gold chain with a small pendant attached.

I pick it up.

Read *Amy* spelled out in gemstones.

I stare at my best friend. Amy is at once a stranger and the person I'd trust with my life. There are no words for my horror at her betrayal.

I dangle the chain. "Missing something?"

"Oh." Amy swallows, pinches her lips. "I thought it came off, um, at Pilates. I was going to go over there this morning to look for it. Josh notices if I don't wear it."

"But it didn't come off 'at Pilates.'" I give the words full air-quotes. "Did it?"

Tears flood Amy's eyes.

"What happened?"

"Keith ambushed me last night. Leaving...the studio. He said he had video of me—you know. He wanted money, or he'd send it to Josh. I told him no, but he just laughed. Said *you* told him how crazy-jealous Josh got. *You* told Keith how much I was afraid of him finding out. *You* said you thought I'd do anything to keep it quiet."

Shitty time for Keith to quote me accurately.

"He'd been watching me. It was easy, he said, because his miserable apartment was only a couple of blocks away." Amy's breath comes in hiccupy gasps. "But I had to give him enough money to screw you out of the house, so he'd have it all to himself."

That bastard. How dare he threaten her. And using my best friend to take revenge on me. I could—

"I pretended to agree. We were right next to my car and it was raining, so I said we should sit inside it to work things out." Amy squeezes her eyes tight for a second. "Getting in my car with him was probably a mistake. Thinking back—cuz he knew I was, like, seeing another guy—I bet he thought I was going to proposition him for his silence.

"But Josh bought me a pistol. For protection. I keep it in a little pocket under the driver's seat. I really only wanted to threaten Keith. Prove that I wasn't some kind of bimbo pushover, but he reached over and..." Her hand goes to her heart. "And he grabbed my breast, started pawing me. It was just this instant—I don't know—*explosion* of rage."

She winces. "Anyhow, I shot him."

"Amy, oh, my God, why didn't you tell me? I would've killed him myself."

"Really?" A split-second tremulous smile spreads across her face; then Amy bursts into tears. "I'm sorry about taking him to your house. I just drove there by instinct. You were the only person I could think of to help me, but...but then I was mad at you, too—thinking, like, none of this would've happened if you hadn't blabbed."

Truth. I race to Amy and wrap my arms around her. Like a parent soothing a hurt child, I murmur, "It's okay; it's okay" to her "I'm sorry; I'm sorry."

Her cries subside into sniffles. Amy steps away from me.

"I shouldn't have just left him. I know you would have helped me if I hadn't been so resentful, if I'd only asked—that's what best friends are for. Plus, it would've made schlepping Keith around so much easier."

I keep patting Amy's arm. "Yeah, how'd you get him onto my porch by yourself?"

"Pilates, baby." Amy thrusts out her shoulders and grins. "It's amazing for core strength. You should try it sometime."

She holds out her hands. In any other situation, she'd be asking me to come closer for another hug. This time, her eyes are on the diamond necklace. "We good?"

No loans. No buy-out. No continuing hassle. "I won't tell if you don't." I can keep the house. And Amy should be off the hook for homicide.

I drop the necklace into Amy's hand. "Deal."

Amy's face loses the tension I've seen in it all morning— tension I'd chosen to chalk up to normal necrophobia, *not* to manhandling the corpse she thought she'd disposed of the night before and guilt over keeping her secret from me.

The tide runs out stronger now. Together, we roll Keith off the tarp and into the water. The east wind whisks him away from the ramp toward the middle of the stream where the water rushes faster. Small waves buffet his body. He's two-thirds submerged and, with more rain coming this cloudy morning, any inquisitive fishermen who might snag an unwanted catch will be home.

Keith floats away, northward. Up Admiralty Inlet. Toward the open Pacific. His body becomes...just a log in the current pushing water out to sea. I don't know where Keith will end up. And as long as it's not my doorstep, I don't care.

☂☂☂

OH, WHAT NOW?
Fran Fuller

T rust your instinct. Listen to your gut."
I could hear the voice of the late, great John Dunning echoing in my head.

I always heard him giving me advice when I was sorting through books that people wanted to sell or donate. Most booksellers do. And those of us privileged enough to have the special classes, the ones that were Dunning-invite only, well, we listened harder than the rest.

You remember John Dunning, right? He wrote the bestseller *Booked to Die* but more than that, he was a book scout of exceptional merit. Other book scouts followed him, noting what he chose. The classes were for people he handpicked. We knew why once we were there. Instinct, intuition. Yeah, that's what we have, apparently in spades. No otherworldly, supernatural shit. Just the ability to find special books. I'm sticking with that.

I'd been waffling about taking in the battered copy of Jerry Ford's *Who in Hell is Wanda Fuca?* I mean it sells, can't keep 'em on the shelf, but this one had seen much better days. But my gut said keep it, so I did, and I smiled as I flipped through it, figuring out how much to price it for. It really was battered, and the corner of the cover was torn off, but I knew someone would want it, even at a buck.

A slip of paper drifted out, and I caught it before it hit the floor, so I was really proud of myself. I'm not usually that dexterous. I opened it up.

"Fuck."

I went back behind the counter and sat down on my chair, turning away from the computer, tossing the paperback onto the sorting table. I read the note again.

Please help! Elliott.

And the little red heart in the corner.

I hated getting these things. Generally, I could ignore them, but once in a while I couldn't. I heard John's words again. Dammit.

Then I grinned. This was gonna take research, and that's not my specialty. That's what a librarian is for, and I knew just who to call. I turned to the phone and just as I put my hand on the receiver, it rang.

"Mayhem and Murder, this is Ellie, how can I help you?"

"I thought I'd save you the trouble," Kat Richardson's voice chuckled down the line. "I know what you have, and no, I can't help. In fact, I was the one who made sure it went to you."

"What?" I scowled at the shop, currently devoid of customers. "You know I hate when you pull that crap. I was gonna at least bring it to you in person. Why can't you help? And why me?"

Kat was my contact at the Seattle Public Library, and she's part of that special network, the group of Dunning graduates. Although I refused to think about how Kat got the note to me.

"How did you know I'd be holding a book?"

She laughed. "You own a bookshop, partly because you love pushing books on unsuspecting people, but partly because you're an addict. You always have a book in your hand."

I grinned. "Guilty on all counts, but I could've been helping a customer. I did just take in some used books, after all."

"Girl, I don't know how you can support yourself, much less pay Jimmy to stick around. You almost always have spare time."

I grimaced. Business was slow, and since construction started in Pioneer Square, it had gotten worse. But tourist season was coming, and we had some heavy hitters scheduled to come in and sign, so I figured we'd be okay. I glanced out the window at the ongoing drizzle and shrugged. People love Seattle, and people love a good mystery. Times were tough, but then, when weren't they? That's what mysteries can take you away from.

"So, what do you know about this note?" I kicked back, my feet on the counter.

"Probably as much as you do." I could hear Kat sigh, and her door close and her chair squeak as she sat. "Look, I got it because these things always come to me. It's the price of being a librarian, and, well, one of us." I heard rustling and knew she was going through her candy stash. "But I glanced at it and knew it wasn't something I should be spending my time on, no offense."

I snorted. "So, it's nothing important? And you sent it to me? Why bother? If it's no biggie, I'll ignore it."

"You won't be able to. I wasn't. I tossed it away a couple of times, but it always came back." She bit into something crunchy and mumbled at me.

"You know I hate it when you do that."

"What? Send persistent but minor problems your way?"

"Well, yeah, that too. But eat something without sharing. I have no idea what you're eating, but now I'm hungry."

She laughed. "You'll be fine. So anyway, do whatever you want, but I think this is something you're going to want to track down."

We chatted for a bit more, and I hung up. I rubbed my thumb over the little red heart on the corner of the Post-it, and shook my head, then shouted for my second-in-command, Jimmy Thomsen. I say second-in-command, but since there are only the two of us, it's not a huge leap.

He poked his head out of the office where I knew he'd say he was working but I strongly suspected he was playing solitaire.

But maybe he was just reading. That's one of the perks of owning a bookshop: reading on the job is often required work. It's tough, but we've gotta keep up with what's out there.

Still, we all go through times when nothing sounds good. Books are like food that way.

"What's up?"

I stood up and stretched. "I've gotta go out, so you've got the helm."

He wandered over, rubbing his stubbled chin. So maybe not solitaire. Maybe napping. Fair enough. "What's up?" he repeated. "Where are you going?" He plucked the Post-it out of my hand. "Huh, where'd this come from?" Then he shook his head. "Never mind, I don't wanna know." He yawned and stretched. Definitely napping. "Anything you need me to take care of? How long you think you'll be gone?"

I pointed at the stack of used books I'd taken in. "Those need pricing. And I have no idea. I could be back in half an hour, or you might have to close. These things take as long as they take, I guess."

Jimmy looked at me shrewdly. "Until it's figured out, then. No problem. Rather you than me. I'm perfectly happy not dealing with your"—I glared, and he grinned—"hunches. I'll hold the fort."

He started sorting while I got my purse and raincoat. I debated taking an umbrella, but it really wasn't that wet, and it'd be just one more thing to carry. True Seattleites pretend that they don't need umbrellas, but everyone has at least two. I reminded myself there was one in the car and headed out.

Seattle traffic is oddly polite while being passively aggressive in its grumpiness. There's no honking, everyone waits their turn, but each car manages to exude an air of extremely put-upon patience. Of course, the rain allows folks to pull the "oops, sorry, didn't see you" wave as they cut you off or almost hit some poor cyclist. It's oddly reassuring.

I pulled out of the Sinking Ship parking lot, hoarding my

parking pass. If I was lucky, the same slot would be empty when I got back, and I could pretend I never left, thereby not paying for parking again. It's the little things in life.

I could just drive around for a bit, pretending that I had no idea where I was going, but it's silly to lie to oneself over something so obvious. I knew "Elliott" wasn't the name of the person who needed help, and there was no sense pretending. I maneuvered my way through the steep, narrow, annoying one-way streets until I could get up and over to Pike and Pine and search for parking by Elliott Bay Books. I'd dismissed taking the bus, since this would be faster if I could just find parking. Fortunately, I drive a tiny car, so I can irritate people by parking in improbable places.

I squelched my way into Seattle's biggest indie bookstore. It's bright and cheerful and always busy. The retail part of my brain is always envious, but I'm also glad I don't have to figure out what to order and how much. Having a specialty shop narrows my options, which is a relief, mostly.

I looked around, wondering where I should go when I saw my friend Kevin O'Brien waving at me, his auburn hair burnished in the light. I went over, removing my raincoat, and we hugged.

"Ellie, I was just thinking about you, and look at you, here you are!" Kevin is always delightful and makes you feel special. It's one of the reasons Elliott Bay Books holds on tightly to him. He can sell shoes to a snake, and the best part is that he's sincere. I'd have poached him, but he's happier in the hustle and bustle of a busy store, and honestly, I barely had enough work for me and Jimmy. But Kevin's enthusiasm is infectious, and I felt better.

"Oh." His eyes got wide, and he looked around. "I really was just thinking about you, and you pop up." He slung an arm over my shoulders and leaned in conspiratorially. "Is it a hunch? It is, isn't it? I should have known." He studied my face. "Is this one I'm supposed to help with? Is that why you're here?

Judy will let me off if you need me. You know Ms. Jance is always open to our adventures!" We looked at each other and then he slumped a bit. "It isn't, is it. This one's all about you."

"Not just me, but it's one I've gotta follow through. I sure hope you catch the next one, though," I groused, and Kevin's laugh pealed through the store.

"Remember the last hunch I got? We ended up at the top of the Needle, on that platform."

"In the rain and with lightning coming in over the water." I shook my head. "You do things with such a flair, my friend, and I hope you rope in one of the others for your next hunch."

All of us who'd been through the special Dunning academy had picked up John's habit of calling our little inspirations "hunches." It was disarming, and no one thought twice about it, and we could laugh off or deflect what we were doing as something quirky and potentially lucky. God knows, John's hunches found him some incredibly rare books tucked into forgotten corners of places no one had ever heard of. So, he followed his hunches and got lucky in his finds, and he had a knack of knowing which of us had the same talent. Nothing psychic about it. Just incredible good luck, and an impulse to follow a hunch. I'm sticking with that.

"So yeah, I don't know why I'm supposed to be here or what I'm supposed to do or look for, but here I am."

Kevin frowned. "And I was expecting you." He looked at what he was doing, which was sorting through books on a cart. He handed me a book. It was a copy of John Straley's *The Rising and the Rain*. "So, do I put this in mystery, in poetry, in Alaska? I have no idea."

I flipped through it, and another Post-it note peeked out from between the pages. I held it up and stared at Kevin. He shook his head. "Nope. It wasn't me. That wasn't there earlier, I swear." Our eyes locked, and slowly I sighed. Kevin gave me a warm hug. "Yes, this is for you. What does it say?"

Together we read "*It's important. Ravenna,*" and that little heart was in the corner again. "Well, Ravenna is obvious," Kevin said. "In fact, I needed to send a couple of books up there for dear Mr. Dickey, so if you don't mind taking them, it'd really help."

Loaded down with a dozen books wrapped in protective plastic, a multi-colored scarf that Kevin insisted belonged to one of their sellers, and a small box of Fran's candies that he also insisted I needed to take with me—trust him, he just knew—I headed off to the wilds of Ravenna and the branch of Third Place Books that lived there.

The hills are what make Seattle beautiful, and the views are amazing from pretty much anywhere, but because of the angry competition between the two founders, getting anywhere is always going to be a challenge, and getting from the busy-ness of Pike and Pine up to the Ravenna district always takes longer than you think it will. I did not eat the chocolates, but only because I planned on hitting the little café inside the shop. I debated between the Mediterranean-dip sampler platter or one of the breakfasts as I dodged and darted into a parking spot in their small lot.

Amber Miner plopped down across the table from me, not spilling a drop of her latte. She's talented that way. "I figured I'd see you soon, so I've been kind of lurking." Yeah, she's one of us.

"I don't suppose I can hand it off to you," I responded grumpily, and she laughed at the hope in my face. But, like Kevin, her laugh is infectious, and I was chuckling myself as I loaded up a warm slice of pita. "No, of course not. So, what do you have? Oh," I said, turning and pulling out the scarf, "Kevin thought this was yours and sent it up, along with a stack of books JB'd requested."

I handed the stack of books to her with the scarf on top, and she nodded as she looked through them. "I don't recognize these, but if Kev says JB wants 'em, then he gets 'em." She ran the multicolored silk scarf through her fingers. "I don't recognize this, but it's lovely." With a shrug, she handed it back. "Dunno, but I don't want it." She paused, then, with much thought, said, "I think you need to hold onto it. It's for later." Her solemn eyes caught mine. "Don't ask me why."

I sighed. Amber's hunches were always stronger than mine. If I was supposed to hang onto it, I would. I started to wrap it around my neck so I wouldn't forget it, but she reached across the table and pulled it off. "It doesn't need hummus all over it." I growled through a mouthful of silky hummus and warm pita, dribbling a bit on my shirt.

"I rest my case."

"Fine." I rubbed at the spot until it blended into the background. There's a reason I wear prints rather than solid colors. Spots are easier to hide. "Besides, it clashes with my shirt."

Amber snorted, then handed me the latest historical book by Sarah Weinman. "I think this is also for you."

I wiped my hands carefully before taking the lovely book. Sarah had written about some of the underrated Seattle women who had strongly impacted crime fiction, and it was on my to-be-read pile. "Okay, but who's it go to? I already have a copy." I started leafing through it. The illustrations were gorgeous, of course, reminding me strongly of Jack Finney's *Time and Again*, but here I recognized the locations.

A yellow Post-it fluttered out and landed next to my baba ghanoush. Because of course. Amber gave me a sympathetic smile and reached for it. "So, this is what you're getting?" She looked at it and nodded. "So, a ferry ride is in your future."

I took the note from her. It read *Bring everything. Eagle Harbor* and had the little red heart on the bottom. "'Bring everything?' What the hell does that mean? How do I know what I'm supposed to be hauling around?"

But I was talking to myself. Amber was nowhere to be seen. I grumbled and mopped up the rest of the dips with the now-cold pita bread. I debated going back to the shop and forgetting all about this silly quest, for about thirty seconds. I knew, though, that I was headed down to the ferry, and pulled up the schedule while I waited. Amber would be back, and I couldn't leave until she did.

I was figuring out the best way to get to the ferry terminal when she popped up next to me, carrying, of all things, a small pet carrier. "What the fuck is that? And what are you doing with it?" I eyed her suspiciously.

"Dunno why you need this, but you do, and Sue at Eagle needs the books inside." She poked a finger through the door. "They're all wrapped up, nice and tight." She gave me a quick fist bump and vanished back into the store.

I spent the drive to the ferry explaining loudly to the universe at large that I didn't appreciate its sense of humor or fucked-up ways of conducting business. If something needed doing, why not just say so? What was up with these stupid hunches and with what was turning into a scavenger hunt, one in which I had no idea what I was looking for or why.

The nice thing about a tiny car is that you get a reduced ferry fare, so I paid, pulled into my designated slot when my turn came, set the parking brake, and hauled myself up onto the deck. I debated going out and standing out in the wind and spray, and decided that was too much nature, so I found an empty booth and stared out at the waves being chased by the gulls.

A long-haired man and his attractive girlfriend stopped by and offered me a burrito they'd picked up while they were waiting to board. I declined, and as they wandered off, I heard her saying, "Seriously, no one is going to want a quinoa burrito. Feed it to the damned birds," and I found myself wondering if birds would eat quinoa. I know I won't.

I spent the rest of the ride pondering what various creatures did eat, and if I was going to be stuck carting around an annoyed cat or yappy dog in that carrier. I didn't think it was possible for my attitude to become more sour, but it turned out that I was wrong.

Sue Transeaux was waiting for me under the awning at Eagle

Harbor Books. She always makes me smile, and again I found myself wondering how it is that so many people with red hair, or at least red highlights, manage to be in the book world. I debated dyeing my hair just to fit in.

I had looked forward to a nice visit with Sue, but she informed me that I needed to hustle back onto the ferry, since Janet Rudolph at Page Two Books in Burien really needed the historical books that Sue had set aside for her and had forgotten to send over last time. She also added four cans of high-protein wet cat food which I figured were for Janet's cats. A quick hug later and I was back in line, grumbling to myself and eating the Fran's candy. I don't know who was supposed to get it, but tough beans. I needed them.

I called Jimmy to let him know what was up. "I figured I was closing," he said, and I could hear the grin in his voice. It took a lot to rattle Jimmy.

"Looks like it." I explained what was going on, and he commiserated. He knows I hate driving in Seattle, and that I can get lost in a heartbeat. It's all the damned one-way streets and inability to turn around when you've missed an exit. Don't get me started on construction detours. No, really.

Back on the mainland, I took back roads to Burien because there was yet another clog-up on I-5, and I just couldn't be bothered. It was about three p.m. when I got to Page Two, and I was tired, damp, and downright pissy. Enough already.

When I got there, Janet had stepped out, but Bob Dugoni gave me a huge hug and a fuzzy mechanical toy in exchange for the books. I stared at him. "What's this?"

"I have no idea. We don't even carry them, but Janet said you needed it, and I'm to give you this as well." Bob handed me what I swear was the same tattered copy of *Where In Hell is Wanda Fuca* that I'd taken in that morning. It even had the same tear on the cover.

"Where did you get this?" My eyes narrowed in suspicion. "You haven't been up to M&M today, have you? Has Janet?"

Bob frowned at me. "Nope. Neither of us has been downtown for a couple of days. Why?"

"Because I took this same book in today, and I swear it's this exact book!" I flipped through it and sure enough, another Post-it popped out. I glared at Bob so vehemently that he took a step back. "You didn't put this in there, did you?"

He shook his head, dark hair spilling over his forehead. "I never would. Why would I? What's going on?"

I sighed and slumped into the chair next to the office door. "I'm sorry. I've spent the day running around, and I'm tired and grumpy and—"

Bob interrupted. "Oh, okay, it's a hunch thing." I nodded, and he said, "Janet's on one too. I'm so glad I don't get those. They seem to be exhausting, but maybe a little bit fun?" I could hear the wistfulness in his voice. I had no answers for him. He might very well have the gift, but with John Dunning off to that great bookshop in the sky, I had no idea who would mentor people with hunches.

"Trust your gut," I said. "It's what we were told. And pay attention to the small things. But mostly, trust your gut." I looked at the note I'd clutched in my hand, smoothing it out. "Huh. Not helpful."

Bring all. PP-2nd Floor.

"Bring everything you've gathered?" Bob tucked the fuzzy toy into my hands. "And I guess Pike Place, second floor? But who's there? I don't know of a bookshop on that level."

I sighed and pushed myself up. "I'll figure it out once I get there, I guess. But maybe this'll be the end of it."

With a consoling pat on my shoulder, Bob turned to answer the phone while I headed back out to my car. I shoved the toy into the carrier, along with the scarf and the cat food. I didn't like where this was heading. I have an aversion to litter boxes. Better not be for me, dammit.

Once again, I was grateful for a small car. Navigating anywhere near the Market is challenging if you're driving, and today was no exception. I ended up parking way below the Market and climbing the stairs to the top, carrier in hand. Because I'm me, I went all the way to the top instead of stopping at the second level like a normal person. But there's something about the vibrancy of Pike Place that demands that you experience that first level, where they're slinging fish, selling flowers and vegetables, and you just have to pet Rachel, the pig.

So, I stood there, carrier in hand, just watching the ebb and flow of people, before I trudged back down to the second level. I had no idea what I was looking for, so I just wandered, and found myself pulled into the game-and-magic store, Wishful Thinking. It was owned by the Gutierrez family, but it was actually run by the dad and oldest son, who was about twelve or so.

In an odd but endearing sort of way, it was the twelve-year-old, Jake, who really ran the shop. Oh sure, his father, Anthony, was nominally in charge, but Anthony was easily distracted, and it was Jake who kept Anthony focused. They both had charisma in spades, so it never surprised me to see the shop flourishing despite the unconventional set-up.

"Okay, there you are. I was getting worried."

I looked down at Jake's smiling face.

"You? You've been waiting for me?"

He nodded earnestly, his toffee hair flopping into his eyes. "It's almost time, and I knew you wouldn't miss it, but"—he grinned—"stuff happens. Are you ready?" He turned and hurried away. I followed quickly because Jake is fast, and he's smaller than average so in the crowd, so it was easy for me to lose him, and I didn't enjoy his patient but irritated face when he had to come find me. It was funny how the adult/kid relationship changed when Jake was around.

I scuttled and wove my way through the throngs to the end of the second level by the stairs going up. Jake stopped in front of me so suddenly that I almost stepped on him, and I did bonk him with the carrier.

"You have a scarf?" He didn't give me a chance to answer but opened the carrier and pulled out the multi-colored silk scarf. "Perfect. Okay, so here's what we're going to do." He spun around. "I'm going to create a distraction. You're going to replace the ferret with the cat toy." He peered up at me through his long hair. "The batteries are charged, aren't they? We can't afford a mistake."

I goggled at him, then pulled the toy out of the carrier. It looked like a ball with a long tail attached, and it wiggled and rolled around. Jake eyed it critically, then wiggled his fingers and new batteries appeared. "Better to be safe, although he doesn't deserve it."

"What are we doing?" I whispered as he switched out the batteries, making the old ones disappear. I've never seen Jake's fingers be still, and his quickness and dexterity made his tricks really look like magic. He's going to be a great stage magician, or a great pickpocket. Maybe both. Maybe he is already.

"We"—he nodded his head toward a nearby cage—"are performing an act of mercy. The guy who runs this stall keeps a ferret in that cage, and he neglects it. It pisses me off, and I've decided to do something." His bright eyes sparkled at me. "You're helping because it's the right thing to do. You're fast and you won't mind."

"How do you know I won't mind?" I looked around at the crowd, then peered closer at the cage. The cream-colored weasel looked incredibly sad. And thin.

"A hunch." He winked. "So, I'll distract folks, including the asshole, and you switch the toy for the ferret. I'll meet you back at the shop."

"Yours or mine?" I was looking at the cage, figuring the best way.

"Mine, duh. Don't be silly. Ready?" And with that, Jake spun away and started up with the silk scarf, picking up things and making them disappear, pulling cards and coins and, where the hell did he get a parakeet? Not a dove or a pigeon, but a parakeet. Oh wait, there's the pigeon, but they're all over the place.

I was mesmerized by his movements until a ball flew out of nowhere and thumped me solidly between the eyes. Hastily, I opened the cage, pulled the listless ferret out, and replaced it with the cat toy, which started rolling around the cage. Without a backward glance, I sauntered off down the hallway, not rushing, pausing to window-shop, taking my time, and ended up back at Wishful Thinking in no time at all.

I wasn't surprised to find Jake already there. I went to the side counter and set the carrier down. The ferret hadn't made a sound, so I poked a finger in to be sure it was still alive. It bit me.

I exchanged hugs with Anthony, who hugs everyone, and told him I had his ferret. He looked at me, puzzled. "Ferret? We can't have a ferret. Jake's allergic."

I turned and stared at Jake. "What?" He grinned at me. "It had to be saved, and you need it."

"I do not need a ferret. I don't even like them. They smell, and they get into everything."

"It's not for you, exactly. It's for M&M." I stared at him in disbelief. He gave me that disarming grin and shrugged again. "I just have a hunch." I scowled at him, but Jake is impervious to my scowls.

I lugged the ferret back to my car and got to Murder and Mayhem just as Jimmy was pulling in the street sign. "Back by closing? Figures." He shook his head. "What've you got there?"

I grumbled and went back into the office, ferret in hand. Plopping the carrier down on the floor, I sighed and looked at the day's receipts. Then I looked again. I heard Jimmy chuckle as he sank into his chair. "Yeah, a pretty good day."

"Good? Are you sure that's right? That's five figures? That can't be right!" I turned and stared at his smiling face. "What did you do? What sold?"

Jimmy leaned back, looking smug. "Janine Wilson took that

Doyle first edition she's been talking about." To my stunned face, he nodded. "Her mother-in-law is coming to visit, and you know how they wind each other up. Janine had to have a one-up trophy, so the Doyle went home with her, and I made her promise that she wouldn't return it once Mummy is gone. It's hers for good."

I whooped and gave Jimmy a high-five. He leaned forward and picked up the carrier. "What have we here?" The next thing I knew, he had the ferret out and was hand feeding it bits of the wet cat food. "So, we have a ferret? Cool! And now we can afford to build a huge ferret run through the shop..." His voice faded as he went out onto the floor, visualizing a series of tunnels around the shop.

I leaned back, closing my eyes. What a day.

"So, your hunch got us a ferret? How did that happen?"

I opened one eye. "Sit down and I'll tell you." I watched him play with the ferret. "What are you going to name him?"

"I was thinking Chaos, since he's probably going to bring plenty, but I think Dash. Dashiell, Dash for short." He held up the ferret and looked in its face. "Yep, he's a Dash."

I grinned. "Perfect, since he was stolen."

"Stolen? We've got a hot ferret?" Jimmy's grin matched mine.

"Yep. And I have a hunch he's going to fit in perfectly. Let me tell you about my day..."

☂

AUTHOR'S NOTES: *On each last Saturday in April, some thirty Seattle-area independent bookstores are celebrated in a huge competition in which participants try to get stamps from all participating indie bookstores, of which Seattle Mystery Bookshop was proudly one. With our skull-and-crossbones stamp, J.B. Dickey, Amber Miner—and whoever else was working that day, including Janine Wilson—and I tackled the "passports" of everyone who played, and that was the basis for this story, on a much smaller scale. If Ellie had to hit all thirty stores, you'd be bored and I'd be even more nuts.*

This story is an homage to Seattle-area bookstores, and a shout-out to a very few of the fabulous authors in the area. All of the bookstores mentioned are real, and you should absolutely visit them.

Many of the people in the story are authors, and you should read their books. G.M. Ford, Kat Richardson, Kevin O'Brien, Judy (J.A. Jance), Robert Dugoni, are all local authors, and Jim Thomsen is best known for his editing prowess. But don't miss reading Sarah Weinman, Jack Finney, Janet Rudolph, or Dashiell Hammett.

We're all indebted to the late John Dunning for his love of collectible books, and his generosity.

There are a couple of other inside moments. The quinoa burrito incident really happened. My son and his wife, along with my wife and I, were on a ferry, and we had a quinoa burrito that not only could we not eat, even the seagulls refused it. It's still an ongoing joke in our family.

The father-and-son duo at the end are not bookshop-related, but they are good friends, and it was Jake himself who inspired this whole story. Our lunches with Jake and Anthony remain highlights, and I'm grateful to both.

☂☂☂

NOTES

Most of the stories in *The Killing Rain* were selected through a blind screening process. Every submitted story—nearly one hundred—was stripped of the author's name and read by a group of screeners (see Acknowledgements). Those deemed the most promising were passed along to me, and I wound up ready more than fifty stories before selecting the fourteen you see here—all before I knew who the authors were. A handful of authors were approached about submitting, and three of them took us up on it (and all were stories I would have selected had they been submitted blind).

Proceeds from sales of *The Killing Rain* will benefit the Page Ahead Children's Literacy Program, which works to close the literacy opportunity gap that too often leaves children in communities of concentrated low income behind. (More at leftcoastcrime.org/2024/Charity.html.) Please give generously, through us, or directly via pageahead.org. Let's get the kids started on crime fiction!

ACKNOWLEDGMENTS

I could not have put this anthology into your hands by myself. For one, I have the executive function of a six-year-old off his ADD meds, and I was exceptionally fortunate to have the highly capable Laurie Rockenbeck keeping me on track with a series of spreadsheets and gentle nudges when I got overwhelmed. Her work—"assistance" seems too subordinate a word—was as appreciated as it was inexhaustible and essential, and I am forever grateful that she stepped up and gave us all a virtual hard slap when it was required during the many thriller-like twists this book took in its journey to the Left Coast Crime table. She carried *The Killing Rain* across the finish line, and this book is as much hers as mine. Thank you, Laurie.

My longtime friends Brian Thornton, David B. Schlosser and Scotti Andrews served as screener readers, proofreaders and, at crucial moments, drink-purchasing pep-talkers.

Another longtime friend, Beth Jusino—the best workshop teacher and developmental editor I know—also volunteered her sharp and discerning eye to the screening process.

Thanks too to Steven Steinbock for his screening work, Leslie Hall and Larry Keeton for their proofreading help, and to Kate Jackson, author extraordinaire and social-media rock star, for her many signal boosts for Seattle Shakedown and *The Killing Rain* across several online platforms. And to Bill Cameron, who not only designed a killer cover but patiently put up with my many Columbo-esque "oh, just one more thing" revision requests.

And to Lance Wright and Eric Campbell at Down & Out Books for giving this book the home it deserves despite my failings and flailings and flushed deadlines.

ABOUT THE EDITOR

JIM THOMSEN is a writer and manuscript editor whose crime-centric fiction and nonfiction has appeared in *Black Cat, Diner Noir, Mystery Tribune, Noir City, Pulp Modern, The Rap Sheet, Shotgun Honey, Switchblade* and *West Coast Crime Wave,* among other publications. A former newspaper reporter and editor, Jim was raised on Bainbridge Island, a ferry ride due west of downtown Seattle, and now makes his home with his wife, Sue, in Kingston, apparently doomed to be held eternally hostage by the state's increasingly schizophrenic ferry system. Jim's interests include noir photography, long walks in the rain (without an umbrella, of course) all things 1970s, and the perpetual suffering of the forever Seattle Mariners fan. More about Jim at jimthomsencreative.com.

ABOUT THE CONTRIBUTORS

SAM WIEBE is the author of the Wakeland novels, one of the most authentic and acclaimed contemporary detective series. His work has won the Crime Writers of Canada award and the Kobo Emerging Writers prize, and been shortlisted for the Edgar, Hammett, Shamus, Independent Publisher, and City of Vancouver book prizes. His latest novel, *Ocean Drive*, is a standalone crime thriller described as "a Pacific Northwest *Fargo*." Wiebe also writes (allegedly) as Nolan Chase, whose first mystery novel, *A Lonesome Place for Dying*, comes out May 2024. More at samwiebe.com.

CAYCE OSBORNE is a writer and graphic designer from Madison, Wisconsin. Her stories have been published in literary magazines, including *Typehouse* and Atlas + Alice, and in short story anthologies, including *Pizza Parties and Poltergeists* and *Monsters Monsters Monsters Monsters*. Her debut mystery novel, *I Know What You Did*, was released in July 2023 by Crooked Lane Books. She is a member of Sisters in Crime, Mystery Writers of America, International Thriller Writers, and Wisconsin Writers Association. When not writing, Cayce enjoys spending time with her family, reading, cooking, traveling, and attempting arts and crafts of all kinds. Learn more—and see pictures of Confetti, her goofy Australian Shepherd—at cayceosborne.com.

ROBBY HENSON is a recent convert to fiction writing, having spent most of his career as a writer and director of feature films, including *The Badge* with Billy Bob Thornton, *Pharaoh's Army* with Kris Kristofferson and Chris Cooper, and *The Visitation* with Edward Furlong and Kelly Lynch. His debut novel *Loud Water* was recently published by Down & Out Books. He received his MFA from NYU's graduate film school and has written and directed dozens of documentaries for PBS and other broadcast outlets around the world. He is a member of the Writers Guild of America. He currently teaches screenwriting at the University of Kentucky and is also Artistic Director of Pioneer Playhouse, a regional theater in central Kentucky, where he runs their outreach program Voices Inside that instructs incarcerated writers in writing and performance skills so as to fight recidivism.

BEV VINCENT's most recent book is *Stephen King: A Complete Exploration of his Work, Life, and Influences*. He is the author of more than 130 short stories, including appearances in *Ellery Queen*, *Alfred Hitchcock* and *Black Cat* mystery magazines, two MWA anthologies and Cemetery Dance. His work has been translated into over twenty languages and nominated for the Stoker (twice), Edgar, Ignotus and ITW Thriller Awards, and he is the 2010 winner of the Al Blanchard Award. In 2018, he co-edited the anthology *Flight or Fright* with Stephen King. He is originally from Eastern Canada but has lived near Houston for over thirty years. In addition to writing, he has had a long scientific career, earning a PhD in chemistry in the 1980s, and has published dozens of scientific papers.

Writing as dbschlosser, **DAVID B. SCHLOSSER** is a frequent presenter, moderator, and panelist at fan, writing, editing, and communications events. He has served on the boards of Editorial Freelancers Association, Mystery Writers of America, and Bouchercon. *Best American Mystery Stories 2020* republished "Pretzel Logic" after it appeared in *Die Behind the Wheel: Crime Fiction Inspired by the Music of Steely Dan*. Since the mid-1980s, his fiction, non-fiction, and journalism appeared in print and online under his and other's names. A Kansan who earned degrees at Trinity University and University of Texas and lived in a dozen states, he now calls the Pacific Northwest home. He lives near Seattle with his wife and their dogs and works as a user experience design leader for a global tech company.

ROZ RAY is a writer, teacher, and builder whose fiction has been published in *Hobart, Tahoma Literary Review, Black Heart Magazine, Animal, Easy Street, Geometry,* and *Medium*. Find links to her work on her website, rozray.net. Born and raised in Seattle, she is currently working on a Prohibition-era crime thriller set in her hometown. When she's not writing or building houses, you can find her on a paddleboard or at the boxing gym.

Fun fact about New Jersey: once you turn eighteen, they can't make you stay. It's the law. (You have to pay a toll on your way out, but it's only a few bucks and totally worth it.) Screenwriter **ROBERT J. BINNEY** escaped the Garden State for Atlanta, where he met and married Kelly, the love of his life. They have also lived in Seattle, Coastal Oregon, Philadelphia, and Sydney before returning to the Emerald City, where she is a philanthropy executive. He is a former management consultant and titan of industry. His nonfiction has most recently appeared in the *Los Angeles Times*.

TOD GOLDBERG is the *New York Times* bestselling author of more than a dozen books, most recently *Gangsters Don't Die* (Counterpoint). His short fiction has appeared widely, including in three collections, most recently *The Low Desert*, and has been anthologized in *Best American Mystery & Suspense*. He lives in Indio, Calif., where he directs the Low Residency MFA in Creative Writing & Writing program for the Performing Arts at the University of California-Riverside.

SMITA HARISH JAIN has short stories published and/or upcoming in *Ellery Queen Mystery Magazine*, *Black Cat Mystery Magazine*, and anthologies for Akashic Noir, Mystery Writers of America, Chesapeake Crimes, and several others. Her stories have been a top-ten selection in the Ellery Queen Readers Poll and been nominated for an ITW Thriller Award. She grew up in Mumbai, India and now resides in northern Virginia, where she works as a business professor. She is a member of MWA, SinC, ITW, CWOC, and SFMS.

CHARLES PHILIPP MARTIN grew up in New York City's Greenwich Village. After attending Columbia University and Manhattan School of Music, Martin took off for a six-year paid vacation in the Hong Kong Philharmonic Orchestra. While in Hong Kong he hung up his bow and turned to writing, spending four years as a newspaper columnist, feature writer and jazz broadcaster. *Neon Panic*, his first novel featuring Hong Kong policeman Inspector Herman Lok, was published in 2011. The second Inspector Lok novel, *Rented Grave*, will be coming out in the summer of 2024. His story "Ticket Home" is also featured in Akashic Books' collection *Hong Kong Noir*. Martin now lives in Seattle with his wife Catherine.

JOHN BOSWORTH is a native of Seattle, where he now lives with his wife and son. His short crime fiction has appeared in *Mystery Magazine*, *Black Cat Mystery Magazine*, *Shotgun Honey*, and anthologies from Down & Out Books. He can be reliably found in one of Seattle's excellent parks, breweries, film festivals, or libraries, or online @John_Bosworth_

HAL GLATZER is a novelist, playwright and performer in New York. His Katy Green mysteries are set in the years just before World War II. His Sherlock Holmes pastiches are set in Victorian/Edwardian times, but his latest novel is set in the present day. In *The Nest*, a husband and wife are suspected of homicide, and forced to solve the murder themselves. So it's a "cozy," but it breaks some conventions of the genre. When Glatzer is not working as an author, he's working as a musician, playing guitar and singing the "Great American Songbook" from Tin Pan Alley and Broadway. More about Glatzer is on his website: halglatzer.com. To contact him, please email info@halglatzer.com.

BONNAR SPRING is the award-winning author of eclectic international thrillers and short stories with morally ambiguous protagonists. A nomad at heart, she hitchhiked across Europe at sixteen, joined the Peace Corps after college, and trekked to Machu Picchu for a significant birthday. After living and teaching overseas, Bonnar returned to the US where she earned an Ed.M. from Harvard and taught ESL. In her spare (!!) time, she cooks meals with difficult-to-pronounce names and hosts the Crime Wave podcast, part of the Authors on the Air Radio Network.

FRAN FULLER has been a researcher and transcriptionist, a dispenser of knowledge, and a shameless hustler in her time. Oh sure, she hides behind the titles of secretary, teacher, and bookseller at (the late and much lamented) Seattle Mystery Bookshop, but make no mistake; even though she's retired to the wilds of New Mexico (where it's harder for her to be tracked), she'll still ferret out secrets, hoard knowledge, and trap you into trying new things if you're unwary.

9 781643 963624